bafflegab

bafflegab

a novel by stan rogal

BROAD
SHEET
BOOKS

INSOMNIAC PRESS

Edited by Beth Follett
Copy edited by Phlip Arima
Designed by Mike O'Connor
Interior photographs by Dave Rogal

Some of the material in this book has been published in the follow- ing periodicals: *Existere, K, Chanticleer, Alpha Beat Soup, Carousel, Peckerwood, Scrivener, Catalyst, Tempus Fugit, Carleton Arts Review, Z-Miscellaneous, OH!, Rideau Review, Conspiracy of Silence, Yak* and *Cataclysm*. Much of the material aired on CIUT FM.

Canadian Cataloguing in Publication Data

Rogal, Stan, 1950-
  Bafflegab: a novel

ISBN 1-895837-79-0

I. Title.

PS8585.O391B33 2000   C813'.54   C00-932234-5
PR9199.3.R63B33 2000

The publisher gratefully acknowledges the support of the Canada Council, the Ontario Arts Council and Department of Canadian Heritage through the Book Publishing Industry Development Program.

Printed and bound in Canada

Insomniac Press, 192 Spadina Avenue, Suite 403,
Toronto, Ontario, Canada, M5T 2C2
www.insomniacpress.com

THE CANADA COUNCIL | LE CONSEIL DES ARTS
FOR THE ARTS | DU CANADA
SINCE 1957 | DEPUIS 1957

ONTARIO ARTS COUNCIL
CONSEIL DES ARTS DE L'ONTARIO

This book is dedicated to my friends and family,
especially my brother Gerry,
who *kicked against the pricks*, then got the hell out.

Bafflegab: *n. U.S. Colloq.* An excessive use of circumlocution in expressing simple ideas, giving instructions, etc. Compare GOBBLEDYGOOK.

Few are made for independence—it is a privilege of the strong. And he who attempts it, having the completest right to it but without being compelled to, thereby proves that he is probably not only strong but also daring to the point of recklessness. He ventures into a labyrinth, he multiplies by a thousand the dangers which life as such already brings with it, not the smallest of which is that no one can behold how & where he goes astray, is cut off from the others, and is torn to pieces by some cave-minotaur of conscience. If such a one is destroyed, it takes place so far from the understanding of men that they neither feel it nor sympathize—and he can no longer look back! He can no longer go back even to the pity of men!
  —Friedrich Nietzsche

I believe that we should read only those books that bite and sting us. If a book we are reading does not rouse us with a blow to the head, then why read it? Because it will make us happy you tell me? My God, we would also be happy if we had no books, & the kind of books that make us happy, we could, if necessary, write ourselves. What we need are books that affect us like some grievous misfortune, like the death of one we loved more than ourselves, as if we were banished to distant forests, away from everybody, like a suicide; a book must be the axe for the frozen sea within us. That is what I believe.
  —Franz Kafka

The only world I know without walls is that of illusion & poetry. For me that is the only liberation. I don't believe man can be changed by outer systems. It has to come from within.
  —Anais Nin

Fragments are the only forms I trust.
  —Donald Barthelme

Time for escape. Time to chew the leg off at the knee &
hobble from the trap. In the quiet of a forest a fox gnaws
though the bone of its fourth & final leg. Soon, it will make
its bloodied good-byes to the steeled mechanism & drag its
body across the needled ground toward the comfort of shad-
ows & the rooting paths of freedom…

This is all patter baby, & can be construed as meaningless. Meaningless patter. Yet, when propped up against something, when juxtaposed, when placed at loggerheads with, say, a wall or a quark or a poem or, even, why not?—THE WORLD—then strange things begin to occur. Certain relationships emerge hitherto unknown & whole realms of possibilities & interpretations reveal themselves; some accidental, some planned, & it is endless & mind-boggling & perhaps (dare we hope?) disturbing.

It is difficult to *disturb* anyone these days. It is even difficult to successfully criticize or insult anyone. I wrote a letter to the editor of a poetry magazine stating what a piece of doggerel the magazine was, & offered objective reasons. The editor replied with an apology for *my-not-having-liked-it* & included a small picture at the bottom of the page of a happy face.

To the editors:
POET AS PATACRITICAL TELEGRAMMARIAN
Received my complimentary copy of X. STOP. Pure caca. STOP. Subtitle: *Academic Back-scratching & Mutual Masturbation Society.* STOP. The *biplane of my love?* More like the D.C. 10 of my libido. STOP. Have guts until the guts come through the margins, said Spicer. STOP. Poems as eviscerated as door-knobs. STOP. Needles like a couple of aspirins you give a kid for a runny nose. STOP. Whatever happened to lust? Castrated at the margins of reason. STOP. This mag & its ilk atavistic as a piece of tail. STOP. Where the word *fuck* comes out *fug* through the miracle of sensory

ink. STOP. Chainsaw my name from your mailing list before I drown in sentimental drool. STOP. Not that all poetry has to be apples bruised beneath the blows of their own tiny fists, only that the taste arises from the actual mastication by mouth, tongue & teeth rather than ersatz—via the eyes, ears & brain. STOP. Enclosed are poems. A final burnt offering. STOP.

The reply:

You understand, of course, why we are unable to publish your letter in our POET AS feature [snicker, snicker] & we are sure that your poems will remedy our deplorable situation if accepted [ho, ho].

They weren't & they didn't. It was simply to rattle their chain. We are all so laid-back. Is it the climate, I wonder? Or the myth that we are the ambassadors of compromise? If I hear the phrase Canadian Demographic one more time, I am going to puke. Are we all so content? Or is the idea of actually dealing with the world as-it-is, of actually communicating, of risking failure & ridicule, as dead as a dodo? FLESH HANGS FROM MY EYEBALLS. I am not a violent person. There is room, here, even, for patter. Running off at the mouth in all directions. If the writing seems automatic, it only seems. My foot is heavy on the clutch & I feel the engagement of each gear. If you're along for the ride, you might as well sit back & enjoy the view 'cause getting there is all the fun.

Wednesday. Hump day. Get up, go to the bathroom, do my *thing*: shit, shower, shave. Not yet quite awake, so simply stand in front of the mirror for a time & stare. Notice a few nose hairs protruding, so grab the scissors & give them a quick clip. Also a long, blondish hair growing from my ear lobe. *Snip!* Not feeling particularly ambitious this morning. Figure I'll pick up coffee & a donut on the way to work. Still staring into the mirror. Yawn.

We are plainly egocentric. We are uninterested in anything which does not clearly contain us or a part of us. I'm here to say—we exist as part of everything & must admit our associations with excrement as well as angels. Poems reflect us like funhouse mirrors in strange & distorted fashions. Have a giggle. Enjoy the gargoyle that squats behind your teeth.

What is the point of language anyway? What is its use today except as a game; except as a whip & chair? We encase ourselves in work jargon & jingoism at the expense & exclusion of other individuals & groups. The more specific & job-related the jargon, the more the isolation. It is fashionable, desirable even, to speak in abbreviations & code-oddities. We create clubs of secret hand-shakers complete with shibboleths. Language becomes ingrained & responses automatic. We must remember that language is a tool we use & not something that uses us. It can simplify & constrain us as fast & as decisively as ethical or social laws. We must be aware & prepared to step outside these fabricated walls in order to question & to communicate in the broadest sense. We are subjects to change, not cast in stone, immutable & enduring.

It is a boring fact that bears repetition: as much as artists & writers strive to discover a more universal & common language, society strives for the opposite— happy so long as the machinery continues to run, deathly afraid of anything that might impede or halt that most fictitious of fat-cat terms, PROGRESS.

13

A few days worth of dirty dishes in the sink. Do I do them now & get them out of the way, or do I wait 'til after dinner? Lemme see... I'm having pasta, so I need the pot & the frying pan (which take up most of the room in the sink, anyway), so I may as well clean everything up now & start over again, after I eat, with a new sink full of dirty dishes. First though, a glass of *vino*, to put me in the right *spirit*, so to speak. Then the dishes, then dinner, then... *whatever*.

I am not attempting to make sense. Of the world or otherwise. I am speaking my mind. Plainly. This is not ART. This is not order, except that it parallels my life. Not in the manner of Time, but in the matter of History. History being concurrent & all-inclusive, I shuck the brown leaves of the dated-what-was in favour of the ripe what-is-or-might-become. Therefore, any connection, any association, any thought or idea, any dream, any fact or fantasy, anything dead or living or dead & living—ANYTHING—that drags itself from background to foreground & upstages this play of the sensorium will have its say. The truth (let it be known) is that I lie. Art undoes itself & language is mirrorly expression. It takes all my strength to lift another page & continue.

I guess Summer's finally here. I'm dressed in nothing but shorts. I've got the windows open. The fan's humming away. Nice to get some fresh air blowing through. 'Course, it means more dust everywhere. Traffic roaring by & all that. I'm having to take a cloth to my CD & tape cases. The stereo's onto very cool, very laid-back Jazz at the moment, soon to be bumped up by some Steve Earle. I'm getting in the mood for a little rockin' Country. Who knows, maybe I'll dust the apartment? 'Course, if I do that, I may as well pull out the soap & bucket & give the whole place a good scrub. Why not? It's gotta be done sooner or later, might as well be sooner. I mean, what the hell else was I gonna do today anyhow?

I have been with women: married women who require security; single women who shun involvement; women who are frightened of their lustfulness, who take me in for an evening, relinquish all reason to the pleasure of the moment, engage in the joys of pure selfishness and, *the-world-be-fucked*, they are going to have a good time, then turn me out at the end like a stray cat. They are content for the next three, four, six, *whatever*, weeks with the tiny reel of contraband film locked in their brains which they roll over & over at their discretion (or not): breakfast with husbands, coffee with friends, shopping at the mall, during exercise classes, in front of the

TV—NON-ADMITTING VOYEURS! PEEPSHOW MASTURBATORS! They roll & re-roll the film & playback or loop until it snaps, until it melts, until the pictures fade & the body demands—DEMANDS— another cartridge tucked & set firmly into the breach.

The next day I too maintain that recognizable, self-satisfied grin & inconstant hard-on, but the details: the sense of touch, of taste, of smell are beyond resurrecting. I confess I am no liver of dreams & memories. The past is not merely gone or forgotten, it never occurred. There is only here & now; the ever-hungry present & I am denied entrance to the box office. I am arriving too early or too late. The gates are barred & only a malfunction in the machinery will allow me admission before the designated time. What designated time? I have not even been granted a dated reservation & must wait out the slow grinding of the stars, the proper alignment of the planets. & what good does it do them, these women, these travellers of celluloid & dust, spending their lives in denial & fear? Will the Earth collide with Jupiter? Will crocodiles dance on their teeth? Will their boring little worlds droop & stick like yesterday's fettuccine? Well, why not? Why not & why shouldn't these things happen?

Busy on the street today. Everyone going shopping, I suppose. I've got shopping to do myself & carry a cotton bag for the purpose. It was nice when I wasn't working full time & was able to shop during the week. Now, I have to fight it out with everyone else. Not so bad, I guess. I try to avoid the malls & prefer to shop at the smaller stores or the street markets. Maybe hit a couple of used book stores along the way. Grab a coffee somewhere. Or a beer. Sit on a patio & read the newspaper. Chill out. Relax. Yeah, that's the ticket.

&

They look at the drawing & are astounded. Really amazed. The tree looks like a tree. The rocks look like rocks. The fallen apples look like goddamn fallen apples. Why this fuss over simple imitation? I thought we buried Plato back in the thirteenth chapter of his *Republic*? If I want to see a sunset that looks like a sunset, I'll step outside the door & gaze at the real thing. I don't need to hang its poor cousin on my wall. Why this bent in freezing life & preserving death? The trick should not be, how much can we *take* for ourselves, but, how much can we *add* of ourselves. Nature is not a photograph. Even the rocks cry out, "Touch me," & would gladly drop toward some unknown & eternal centre if given the opportunity.

Clothed in the tatters of ghosts. Yes. It is disgusting. To act disgustingly, obscenely & to be sober. Aye, there's the rub! To lack a credible excuse. Not three sheets to the wind. Ghosts failing to stand up to the scrutiny of microscopes. Worse, they fear the culture. Insanity is a romantic alternative, but difficult to prove before reasonable judges. Bodies must be produced & paraded, each with their severed limbs & reeking of post-mortem intercourse. It is not enough to speak to the dead or wear their skins. No ghost of a chance for us poor, gum-sucking moderns. No bark. No bite. Alas, we are all so fucking reasonable & so fucking boring. Did I say that? I did. I do. These are my opinions & you may feel they have no more importance or interest than a speck of fly shit sucked up in a tornado.

Even to write *nothing*—the word. Nothing. Nothing. Nothing. Nothing. Nothing. This helps. Nothing. Nothing. To scratch the surface of this page with nothing, in defiance of Lear's "Nothing begets nothing," & ending with egg on his face. Or ink. Nothing, a young animal nosing aimlessly, printing a record of paws & excrement. Nothing, a metaphor for nothing & its image. Nothing ventured nothing gained. Nothing, a trail leading to nothing & stopping at nothing. Nothing, an optical illusion of fading impressions pasted to the backs of

speeding cartoon characters. Nothing, the pattern formed by birds as their flights slowly curve from sight to nothing. Nothing to speak of. Nothing to say. Nothing to fear. Nothing. Nothing. Nothing...

The true story of Mr. & Mrs. Frufraw & their two children Billygoat & Puss Puss. Two children not three. A boy & a girl. Perfect symmetry. Half a child less than the National Average but not so awkward, a one for her, a two for him. As a precaution, both Mr. & Mrs. have had the operation. As a precaution, they had each other's operations & things were found to cut & things were found to tie. One can't be too sure. Two less sure. To be absolutely sure, they have given up sex completely & why not? The time it took, the bother, the energy required, the noise, the mess, the apologies for taking too long or coming too soon, the planning for the right time of the month, not to mention the embarrassment of having children (two, a boy & a girl) in the next room & how it would affect them in their later lives consciously &/or subconsciously, the cost of analysis now & later— no, better to end it now while perfectly symmetrical & how much happier can one family get? Better not to take any chances (though the National Average looms). Greed can only end in disaster. Better to maintain & keep what one has got, best to be one hundred percent

positive, Mrs. with the knife held high & Mr. ready; Mr. with the plaster mixed & Mrs. ready afterward to wrap the children (two, a boy & a girl—Billygoat & Puss Puss), in aluminum foil and put them on ice, in the freezer for keeps &, "We are a lucky, lucky little family & happy ever after. Happy ever after. Oh so happy ever after." THE END.

It's late. Not *too* late. Not three in the morning or anything like that. More like eleven. Late, but not too late. I feel like having a cold beer. I mean, why not? The apartment's still hot, I haven't been able to sleep that well anyway, & I feel like having a cold beer. It's funny, if I was out or if I had friends over, it would still be considered early & the idea of having a beer wouldn't be an issue. I'd just have one. But, I guess because I've been sitting here alone at my desk all evening, it seems somehow not-quite-right. So, I toy with the idea. 'Course, I toy with the idea standing in front of the fridge, which pretty much settles which way the decision is going to go. I'm in the mood. I'm thirsty for a cold beer. I open the fridge & pull one out. I twist off the cap. I drink. No big deal after all. I walk over to the window & lean on the ledge. I stare into the sky. It's clear, the stars are bright & I can make out the Little Dipper. There's a crescent moon sitting way up high. I drink my beer. I listen to the

sounds of traffic merge with the music from the stero. It's nice. It's a beautiful night.

It has become pointless to pose the question: *what do I expect?* I expect nothing. Whatever happens, happens. I can live with that. I rather like it. It leaves everything so open-ended, possible & delightfully frightening. Like a child who hesitates before opening the door—one never knows & is glad of the uncertainty. Too soon we sweep the monsters from beneath the beds & shoo the shadows from our closets.

I have also dropped the phrases, *I deserve* & *I'm entitled* from my vocabulary. It seems useless to measure when my terms are never less than life & death. My thinking becomes more abstract & less communicable, directly. I travel in the ear of a purple rhinoceros & even this exceptional beast is unaware of my existence. My typing does not provide enough buzz to raise a tickle.

The first trick to becoming human is to drop your humanity. I mean drop it! Without a second thought or a tear, drop it to your feet like it was a paper bag full of yesterday's stinking garbage. I mean, rid yourself of it! I mean, kick it down the stairs & turn your back! I mean, really leave it behind & forget about it! I mean, forget it! FOR-GET-IT!

I bought a basketball a couple of weeks ago. Nothing fancy, just something cheap that would do the job & now I figure I'll head over to the park & toss it around a bit.

It's early & I've got the court to myself. I'm pretty lousy to begin with (it's been awhile), & I'm bouncing it off the rim of the hoop or missing altogether, but I start getting the hang of it &, pretty soon, a few shots are hitting the mark.

It's fun. The sun is rising & I'm working up a sweat. I take off my T-shirt. I'm pretty awkward, I know. The timing's off & the legs & feet are out of sync. It's hard to get into a rhythm. It doesn't really matter, though. It's not as if I'm planning to turn pro. Just keep at it. *Just keep on keepin' on*, as they say.

In time, I begin to forget my body. I shoot & chase, chase & shoot.

& so I told her, "We are saying the same thing, only we say it differently."

& so she said, "If that's true, try saying it my way." *Ouch!*

It's their involvement with trivia that pisses me off. Their way of turning picayune, little things into *raisons d'etre*; to be aggrandized to a point where it will get them through the day with some feeling of accomplishment, so that when it ends, they can put up their feet, turn on the tube & R E L A X without feeling guilty by the possibility that they are wasting their time, that they *have* wasted their time, that they will waste their time again & are actually ignoring & avoiding anything more complex than preparing a full dinner complete with favourite muzak (something restful, something mellow, something light) & a *good* escape novel. Escape? Leaping lizards, what escape? To where? From what? Wanting to bury oneself in the muck, to escape below rather than above, to live like a mole with blinders rather than a winged dragon. Not so bad to cover oneself with shit to cure dropsy, but to simply cover & hold one's breath? & then to perfume in order to hide the smell from others?

Then to leap up & shout, "What fun! What fun!" & isn't it? Isn't it fun to build the trap, set it, then enter & spring it? Convict yourself to a life behind bars. Good, solid bars cast & constructed from your own two hands. I stick out my tongue, shove my thumbs in my ears, waggle my fingers at passersby who bump into each other, lower their heads, conceal their faces & apologize most apologetically, though unsure as to why or for what & stagger on continuing the same polished pantomime. What a gas! What a lark! What a freak show!

I am sorry. I apologize for being an asshole, & a third-rate asshole at that. It is circumstance that drives me to this, or worse, fate. LIFE IS A TROMBONE. With its finite stops, infinite variations & particular melodies. Very particular & heaven help anyone who gets their head jammed in the slide. My problem exactly, pal. Shall we order another round? There is a will (or a won't) at work here, & the notes have been written.

I read somewhere that Hemingway wrote standing up. I think I read it. I think it was Hemingway. It doesn't matter. Some famous writer wrote standing up & I'm almost sure I read it & I'm almost sure it was Hemingway. Interesting. The word leaked (as words are wont to do) & immediately thousands of would-be writers were on their feet. Picture it. It made sense. It allowed freedom of movement. Energy coursed through the body unimpeded. The blood rushed. It was easier to breathe. Physical stimulation equated mental stimulation & so harmony between mind and body. A sort of metaphysical massage leading to greater inspiration & creativity. So ran the theories. The truth, of course, is that sitting for long periods of time resulted in blisters on the ass. The writer had a tender ass & blisters were an occupational hazard, like tennis elbow or black lung.

My, how willing & desperate we are to grab at any

vagrant straw. How desirous we are to romanticize any simple action without first questioning the possible cause. How quickly we uplift or condemn. *The Theatre of Cruelty* was devised by Antonin Artaud who suffered cancer of the bung-hole & who died insane. Now, there's some romance!

You never know what sort of animal you have created until you flip it on its back & slit open its belly. If only air escapes, you have not succeeded. Even the most attractive skin must be reinforced with bone, muscle, blood & entrails in order to survive. & then, it should not remain a motionless target into which a dull reader might easily sink their teeth. A poem or prose piece should actually defend itself; crawling across the page, waiting in ambush, it must be prepared to spring out, to claw the eyes, genitals & mind. To kill, if necessary.

You've got to do it—choose between what you want to do to maintain your freedom & what you should do as society's slave. Certainly there are losses & you suffer, but you suffer doubly living the life secured by others, your mind forever dwelling on *what if?* & *if only I'd done such-&-such*. What's more? The end is the same except for attitude: finally, you drive your skull into a tree or into the auto dash & just before or at the same instant you regret that the end will be dull & heavy like the split & crumble of concrete; that you'd rather (& wish to!) explode & flame like the volatile-floating Hindenberg— roaring, spectacular & beautiful.

Throw away your vocabulary, dammit, & begin to speak! Quit hiding behind your language as if you invented it. You didn't. You gathered it wholesale at a used car auction. You drive it & put up with its faults because you refuse to spend the money or feel you lack resources. Then junk it, friend! Be honest at least, & recognize the heap as scrap. Don't name it for any reason: Bertha, Baby, Windjammer, so that it becomes real. It is not. A broken mirror. An afterimage. An abortion that swirls at the surface of the toilet.

Unfucking believable! Not bad enough I earn *below* what's considered the poverty level in this country, now the government tells me I owe them more money for last year's taxes. & yet another fucking rejection slip from yet another fucking magazine & (I can't believe it) I cut myself on the fucking envelope. I'm fucking bleeding! I can't believe it. I think I'd better just go outside & take myself for a long walk. & try not to break my leg in the process.

&

Brahe had the right idea. When they cut off your nose, stick a gold one in its place. A class act. One man—an American—sent his eye patch to France. He requested an eye painted on by Matisse, & the eye did not resemble his eye at all, but it was, nonetheless, & perhaps more so, his eye.

"Question not the need." Lear again. Again Lear. Precisely why Art exists—there is no need for it. Food, Shelter & Sex continue to top the charts. Coming right down to it though, what need is there for anything? Isn't everything we do simply a distraction from what everyone knows to be the truth? Life is a bore, baby, & meaningless! We fill time & in the final analysis, what does it matter how that time is spent? Sit on your ass, paint a porch or write a poem, we are filling the void. Nothing more profound. People in search of *themselves*. What the hell does that mean? You are YOU, that accumulation of actions, thoughts & feelings with a potential to fertilizer. Finito. We must be involved with BEING. When the sage says, "GO," it does not mean to some place. There is no *some place* or *one place*, there is only here & now & what we bring to it.

The unsuspecting world being one huge litter box, I go about my business unashamedly—the leanest fat-cat dropping splendiferous gifts without so much as a paw stroke in the sand to apologize or conceal.

Sitting here drinking a cuppa Nescafe. Shoulder sore from shooting too many baskets. Back smarting from too much sun. Now my lower eyelid is twitching. What's that all about?

Partaking of the ultimate experience. Beyond Zen & its entering-into-becoming-one. To do a thing & to observe the doing simultaneously. As if filming yourself, you are the actor & the recorder. You perform the old horror trick of looking up & recognizing yourself in two places at once. Think about it. You stand on the shore while others swim. The sun is setting behind the mountains & shadows are mingling with the light. You'd like to join in the swimming but you don't want to give up the vantage of the shore. You must choose one over the other. Either way there will be some loss. How much better to develop the actor's craft, the ability to transcend realities via the objective eye. To portray many parts at once & make them breathe with life. To step outside & judge; to remain inside & feel. The actor's craft. The human craft.

So you scribble down whatever it is you scribble down—words, phrases, nonsense—then, later, paste it together in your poetry. You've made the connections. Not for *you* the poet. For *you*, the connections were always there because they are YOU. I mean, for the reader, who is without the decoding book, the pocket translator. You make the connections for them, the correspondences; you make the disparate a whole. Which doesn't mean explanation. It is something less formal,

more loving & attuned to the heart & guts than to the mind, but also for the mind in abstract. The poet offers hints of entrances & allows the readers to make their own discoveries. If these discoveries are far from what the poet intended, so much the better. Poems should never be precisely delineated highways, they should be mirrors to fall into almost by accident, though not without a certain amount of seduction & cunning on the part of the poet. Exploration should take the form of an archaeological dig with ghosts for guides.

A poem is dead without an audience. It lies in bed with its maker & they are the same. They can't even talk to each other, never mind get aroused. It is embarrassing & frustrating as hell. This is why a poet should never say, "See how clever, clever I am," when an audience responds to a poem. It is the audience that deserves congratulating. The poet provides some X & Y, while it is the audience that colours in the remainder of the picture with various A to Z & their relations. & if the poem is judged genius or criminal, or genius & criminal, there is nothing for the poet to do except use the information & advance.

The bear hibernates in the palm of my left hand. I keep it closed—the palm—clenched like a cave, the tangled roots of a sumac. SIX MONTHS! containing this black beast, six months allowing it to roam freely the grubby terrain, nosing out sweet berries, pawing ripe salmon from the fat streams. SWIPE! into my toothy palm—EAT! EAT! My palm reeks of blood, shit, urine. Furballs choke the slender lifeline I have, the mange & lethal ticks gnaw my flesh. My coat discolours shaking needles, nettles, dust, insects, sweat; my teeth yellow, I am packing an extra two-hundred-twenty unseemly pounds on my once visible rack. MY WEIGHT DRAGS ME DEEP INTO THE CAVERN OF MY PALM!......... there to dream light dreams six months &, again, float open, like a newly sprung trap.

Someone sharpens a finger (God?) & points. ZAP! A poet lies dead at the bottom of an elevator shaft. Is this a metaphor or cold fact? Where would the elevator go except maybe to the top floor—which is never the poet's—& no further? Some impotent metaphor. The elevator (like the poet) never travels past the top floor though each would prefer to. The momentum seemingly achieved, but travelling against the strength of the design. The infernal, unyielding concrete of it.

Haven't been woke up by this dream in a long time. Used to happen a lot when I was a kid. I'm leaping off a barn roof, arms spread, like I'm going to fly. I do manage to glide for an instant, but that's it. No matter how hard I struggle to keep in the air, to fly, I can't do it. I glide softly downward & land, uhurt, my belly pressed to the ground.

&

Cold comfort of half-lives. We cling to our books. Our poems. Our stories. Our lies. Content against a world neither ordered nor disordered. IT IS. No use to try to go around. Forehead full tilt to the wall. The pain begins & ends, ends & begins, or else it is ceaseless degrees. Scaled very much like a fish. A melody. A mountain.

The pencil drags across the page leaving nothing but language. Better a picture of a tree or a bird; better yet, an image which evokes endless associations. No. Only language with its boring entourage of tacky convention-eers smoking cheap cigars, grinning behind their name tags & puking on the floor.

You have to make the leap. When I say I want to fuck you, you must realize that I do not think of you simply as a cunt or a toilet. If it was just a fuck that I was after I would be more general. I would say, "I want to fuck," or "I want to fuck her," or more generally *any* her. Not so. *You* makes it imperative. You drive me to make the language basic & total. I ache. I want to fuck you.

"To never contradict oneself is to say nothing."— Unamuno

It's always a bit strange when my mom calls. I have to make that mental shift back to an earlier life. Not that the other life was bad, it wasn't. It was just different. The call does, however, often make me question the choices I made that got me here in the first place. Next, there's the readjustment period, & whatever strangeness goes along with that.

I have no past. People laugh when I say this. I have no past. The laughter continues uncomfortably. Not because the phrase appears impossible (which it is); no, the discomfort arises from something much more frightening. To have no past is to abandon all responsibility, all debts, all blame. To have no past is to deny friends, family & even oneself. To have no past is to admit chaos & displacement. Worse than a shipwreck—there is no ship, no storm, no sea. Nothing. Nothing fixed. Everything up to question & examination. Which explains my amorality. *The laws which directed the past are good for the past, they are not necessarily good for the present.* That was Artaud. Is there anything that is motionless? Yes. The flying arrow is motionless. The only change is change. Zeno. Heraclitus. The Greeks had a word for it.

People travel. Back & forth to Europe, Asia, Africa, they travel passive as cheap postcards with nothing to substantiate their visits but the stamp marks which eventually percolate into the cardboard & disappear. What use are photographs except to show the separateness of these tourists from their surroundings & so must be labelled: *Tom beneath the Tower of Pisa, Helen on the steps of St. Mark's Cathedral* or *Larry at the top of the Eiffel Tower?*

I want to enter the world like overripe fruit—slightly stinking, skin soft, flesh ready to be bruised & scarred by everything I see or touch. We must seek deep impressions which can never leave us, which must remain past soap & water & time to remind us of the acts of our excursions & not simply our thoughts; the cuts & welts that read even in the dark like books of brailled phosphorus which burn & penetrate to our very hearts & brains.

Like going to New York to be part of New York. As though one could, New York being more than the total of its inhabitants & buildings; more than a piece of land near the water; more than a visit to Coney Island, the Statue of Liberty or Broadway. & we are astonished at our own disappointment, "I was in New York, but I wasn't. *I* wasn't New York."

Learn this: we can only be part of part of anything & not the thing-in-itself. From a cog to a wheel to a frame to a car—the car is disappointed! As New York, the city, is disappointed because it is not New York the dream, the myth, the *Big Apple*. As we are also disappointed at being only a part of ourselves, only visitors in our own bodies without identification, without guides, without

anything of value to purchase our passage, without any knowledge of a destination. We must travel constantly at great risk & there is so much territory to cover, so many barriers to tear down, so many illusions to shatter.

Again today: I WILL quit smoking. WILL quit drinking. WILL quit carousing. WILL quit drugs. WILL quit swearing. WILL. CAN. MUST. These words & a sense of urgency. A desire, no—a NEED!—for order, health & harmony. Certainly my body & mind rebel against these vices & I know—I KNOW—that I could/would/should quit, & yet, why? I mean, *really*, why? I mean, if I were told that in a few days, one day, better still, that in the next five minutes my lungs would collapse & rot or my legs drop off or I'd go insane or die for Chrissakes then it would be no abstract laughing matter & maybe, YES!— quit immediately & be saved. But to worry some ten, twenty, thirty years down the road & just a chance to be one of the unlucky bastards? No, I'm sorry (& will, likely, be sorrier, yes, later). It can't be done.

I won't be trapped so easily! I've moved my bed within arm's reach of a door. & that's not all. A door stands like a sentry beside the kitchen table, while another door crouches like a sniper behind the captain's bench. I have numerous doors. I have doors of all shapes & sizes: rectangular doors, triangular doors, square doors, octagonal doors, circular doors, doors shaped like stars, doors shaped like keys, doors shaped like the eyes of cats. Some doors are hidden like spies & many are sore-thumb obvious. I have doors big enough to swallow me & all my possessions while others are so tiny I have to squeeze through oiled & naked. Doors sit on either arm of the sofa like carved lions & a door broods below the coffee table like a clam. There is a door, bold as brass, adjacent to the television & another door disguised as *The Last Supper* alongside the fireplace.

There are ceiling doors & wall doors & window doors & floor doors & doors within doors. There are false doors. There are doors containing false doors & false doors containing doors & false doors containing false doors. I know every door, its combination & location. I have implanted doors in tables, chairs, telephones, toasters, fridges, ranges, bathtubs, toilets, TV's, stereos—even books! I carry a door in each hand & attached to each knee, each elbow, each foot, the back of my head & the tip of my nose. DOORS! When it comes time to go—I'm gone!

It was a perfect tanning sun & her body revolved like the exact shadow of a sundial, soaking every drop of ultraviolet.

"Heliotropic," I mumbled.

"What?"

"You're heliotropic. I swear."

"I'm flattered. What is it?"

"You follow the sun. Like a flower."

"Oh. *That* heliotropic." She was beyond calculation. Her body shifted to 4:18 without missing a tick.

One night we'll find ourselves walking down a moon-lit alley. Best of friends. Maybe a thousand years gone or more. Rats will quit their midnight rummage & glare with diabolical yellow eyes. We'll be at opposite ends of the alley striding toward each other. Gunfighters itching to draw. The rats can taste blood. Don't get me wrong. The story may be cockeyed but the guns are real. We're there to kill each other, *fer sure*. Everything comes full circle. A flipped coin aches for fifty percent. Everything aches for balance, neutrality, entropy, death. It's never planned, you know. It arises from necessity. The rats understand & are patient. The moon is uncaring. The one sad part is that one of us must go on living, & it is not the act, but the hollowness that eats away.

Hangin' around the twenty-four donut shop. The street lights are on & the traffic has slowed. Coloured leaves skitter across the sidewalk, being blown by the wind. I'm making little chicken scratches on a coffee stained napkin.

What's more important—that which is said or that which is not said? All of these words are only used to suggest what can't be said. Face it. If I want to say *I love you*, I'll say it straight and simple. These are the words. *I love you*. They issue easily. What is not so easy is the idea, the feeling, the truth of *I love you*. Its completeness. Its actuality. Its physicality. The gentle warmth of one hand enfolding another. These actions speak awkwardly & require effort. They are the blind person's skill to feel beyond the cane, beyond the curb & if one stubs a toe or scrapes a knee or bangs an elbow or bloodies a nose in the attempt, then one is at least aware of being a live & functioning human being—no matter what the outcome: a red herring, a dead end, or (sometimes) a passageway.

Something about the Fall weather. Time for change & all that. I don't know. I'm looking at my face in the mirror, checking out the lines & such. I'm thinking, good thing I'm rehearsing a play tonight. I can be someone else for awhile.

"Aieeeeeeee..."

Ahh, that feels better. Do you think it is an easy thing to perform before a crowd of strangers (& believe me, when it comes to laying one's guts out to bake, everyone is a stranger sporting a knife, fork & bib)? To offer one's insides up for inspection & criticism? It has been said of my writing: *it is too abstract for the everyday reader*. Well, perhaps it's not the level of writing, but the level of the everyday reader that requires investigating, eh? Present company excepted, we are as clear as crystal balls.

Ariadne, my fuzzy spider, drop me a line! Thread this open I that loves you one last time. I'll be good. Honest. I'm through exploring the natural carvations of a wormy mind. I want to come home. Coax me back to your well-ordered web of tender kisses & I'll suck each hair of your many legs. Forgive your poor Theseus. You must know that my thing with the Minotaur was the result of a simple failing—he was grotesque & rough with me! What could I do? I am a victim as much as you & I suffer doubly knowing it is all my fault. Pity me, trapped with this ill-mannered beast; being poked at & slobbered over; having to clean and cook for him. I would kill him, but then where would I be? Not only lost but lonely as well. Ariadne, my fuzzy spider, drop me a line! Thread this open I that loves you one last time!

My mind is full of juice. Piss & vinegar. I am writing through delirium. Not the time of drunkenness, but the few days that follow. The drying out period. When the smoke & alcohol is busily cleansing the brain & body of accumulation. Dog-tired days causing fits of nightmares & hallucinations. The time when one writes because one has to, is forced to. There is no choice, no other way to rid the demons & save yourself. SAVE YOURSELF! The bright key! Salvation through works & you are God & the Devil arm wrestling for a life & you emerge reborn! A human being devoid of everything except yourself. Full of yourself—like a stone is full of stone. Sparkling, naked & alone!

In order to secure some higher level of consciousness, of being, one must first experience complete degradation. It's a sort of a dialectical imperative between your hypothetical self & its antithesis. The process is recurrent & inescapable. It is necessary to discover what one is *not* in order to arrive at what one *is* & may *become*.

I played a number of sports as a kid & something I always remember is that, while I was normally considered a *good* player, I never really achieved greatness. & I don't think that ability, or the lack of it, was entirely to blame. I think that I had the ability just as today I have the ability. No. It has something to do with uniforms. They always feel too big for my body. Or they hang wrong. Or they cling in odd places. You know the difference when you see someone & you say, "Nice uniform. Nice fit." & it is & you can't deny it. It looks right. Meanwhile, I'm at war. I feel uncomfortable. Awkward. I'm too afraid to walk, never mind strut my stuff, running, zigging, zagging on or off the field.

Nothing has changed. I bang away at the typewriter & call myself a poet & I think I look just as much like a poet as anyone else. Still, they look good up there pitching while I warm the bullpen. They throw their fast, fast balls, their curves & their sliders without a ruffle. I have those plus knuckle & screwball. But the second I move, the instant I leave the darkness and enter the light my shirt untucks, my shoelaces untie & my socks droop around my ankles. I am not a pretty sight & the laughter is uncontrollable & increasing. I don't blame the crowd. In a different position I would laugh as well. The courageous thing would be to play without a uniform; to appear naked in the hope of being recognized & applauded on the strength of my arm alone; on the basis of my performance rather than the correctness of my costume. But is it done? Would the crowds approve? Would I be sent to the showers, fined, even suspended—banished for eternity not merely from the game but from the ball park as well? I don't know. The shoes pinch &

the rough collar chaffs my neck. I think about it. I am
thinking about it.

The weather is not too bad, though threatening. I'm
taking advantage of the day by shooting a few baskets.
I've gotten better able to play the game & think about
other things at the same time, without tripping over my
feet. This can be a good or bad thing. Uh oh, a gang of
spike-leathered clouds are kicking the shit out of my
blue sky. Time to circle the wagons & head the hell
home.

The chair stands perfectly still in the middle of the
floor &...well? Go ahead. Sit. It's waiting. It calls to you
as only a chair can: complete chairness & you believe it.
The chair is an invitation with your name on it, an invitation to sit & so you will. Never a thought that this
chair may actually be a paid assassin in disguise or that it
is haunted by the blood-stained ghost of Lizzie Borden's
axe or that a moment ago it was a lowly cockroach & an

hour from now it will transform itself into a majestic winged serpent & swoop out the door. Sit! Go on! You've categorized it—CHAIR!—that makes it safe. & yet...it has those clutching arms, those quivering legs & as your body lowers, you freeze, catch yourself listening for the smack of lips, the click & grind of teeth, the meaty exhalation of a well-formed lung.

Why did I have to be born beautiful, talented & brilliant? Why not the opposite? Equipped with just enough solid stones in my craw to pave the way mindlessly toward death. Happy & at peace.

I guess it's time to write a goddamn novel. Poetry doesn't pay. I mean real poetry. Poetry that threatens, brutal as an ice pick or gentle as fog; able to conjure visions that seduce people to abandon their safe lives & voyage into the unknown toward never-never land.

I'm not blaming anyone. It's not a trip for the faint of heart nor the weak of stomach. It is not a well-packaged plan. It does not fit neatly into a two hour TV or theatre program. Poetry requires the participation of the self & there is no room for armchair audiences.

James Dickey gave up his high paying job as an adman for Coca-Cola in order to concentrate on his poetry. Imagine the raised eyebrows. His friends tried to understand. They almost begged him. "Listen, Jim, we like your poetry & as a *hobby* it's fine, BUT, if you really want to throw away your life in an attempt to MAKE IT as a writer, then you really have to be a novelist. People respect novels. They're long and complete. They tell a story."

So, Jim loaded an arrow into his crossbow, aimed & (in his finest down-home, good-boy, country-fried-mammoth-voice) said, "Hell. Any idiot can write a novel."

ZING! He wrote *Deliverance*, & the rest, don't y'know, is history.

Hum: *What the world wants today, it's the real thing.*

Auntie has three inch fingernails which never curl & never split. She files each one stilleto-sharp, then paints—scarlet, orange, lilac, indigo, emerald. Never all the same; variegated, prismatic, reflections of mood or whimsy.

Indelicate as they first appear, Auntie controls them, not as tiny machines, but as extensions of her already long & tapered fingers. Just as a chef's knives act as a part of him, so Auntie's nails gently excite the murmur of the cat or casually strip the peel from a grape.

During moments of remembrance she pauses by the fireplace & a golden nail traces the outline of a young man in uniform.

When she masturbates she wraps them in coloured scarves & when she makes love, her nails dance like dove's feet across the flesh.

If I say *woodpile* & you think *capitalism* then you deal in metaphor. You have trained yourself to see past the visible. You have, though, completely missed the wood-pile. You have trained yourself to see exactly what you want to see. You have cut yourself off. You see past the visible to the visible, & you miss the woodpile.

I'm reading a magazine & there's this reprint of a Norman Rockwell painting. It's a mother baking pies & the kids & neighbour kids & pets & a minister are all hanging around waiting for a slice. It brought back some memories. Not that my childhood was anywhere near the Norman Rockwell world, just that there were days like that, with my mom churning out pies & tarts & loaves of bread, meant to keep the family going while she went to work during the week, or into hospital, pregnant with another little brother or sister.

She sits at a table folding daffodils like old, worn coveralls. The action is automatic, as though she were the final stage of a floral assembly line. She has acquired a style, a rhythm & any break in order results from a defect in the makeup of a particular flower—it's physicality. She accepts no blame personally, since she has no outside connection either with its beauty or smell, nor does she make associations regarding dreams & memories. She doesn't care. The fact is obvious in the handling: leaves crossed in front, a fold made in the stem's middle, excess tucked into the fold, the yellow bloom pressed flat & open. Each one identical. The daffodils are meaningless to her. They have been together too long or she prefers roses or someone has died beyond the aid of daffodils. They are yesterday's news. Nothing remains but

the activity of her hands, a formula requiring repetition without thought. She folds daffodils & places them in the drawers of books. The books she aligns perfectly on shelves not-to-be-tampered-with-penalty-by-death. The reason eludes her. It is enough to perform & believe.

There is nothing out of sync in this room. Shelves fill the walls, books cover the floors, daffodils arrive by the bucketful & the woman folds & stores. There is enough to last a lifetime. Strict, efficient & functioning like a well-oiled mangle, it is her world & if she has any secrets, they reside between leaves of books, trapped in pockets of golden daffodils.

Everyone wants to sell me something. They knock & they ring. I am tired of explaining. Tired of refusing. Tired of being polite. The work does not write itself. Now when they try the door, I greet them banging a spoon to a metal pot; I sing arias. When they phone, I crank up the Beethoven or recite poetry. It's too bad that most of my victims are innocent pawns, but the guilty are beyond reach. They shoot craps somewhere in the bowels of Kafka's hat.

Dear editor:

Ain't it grand! For all us knuckleheads who avoided the jogging tracks & racquetball courts—fresh blood! The word is from science & the word is good. For freedom from stress pursue the married life & callisthenics of the brain. Newly forged keys to a longer, happier & healthier existence. Settled academics, come out of your ivory tower boudoirs & proclaim your secrets! The world knocks & will not be refused a better mousetrap. The mind boggles! Witness a second golden age of cerebral centenarians, gray-skinned artists & philosophers. Break out the Kierkegaard, Martha; take the leap of faith. It's nose to the page & two feet from the grave.

What? No takers? Then how about education as a contact sport?

It can sound very romantic, I suppose. "He supported himself as a maintenance person while performing his Art on the side." To some innocent one hundred years from now (me long-since dead & buried), it can afford to sound romantic. Very romantic. Like insanity or suicide. But to me now & alive, no! It is not romantic. It is a drag & a damn shame. I want to pay my way with my *works* like any carpenter or bricklayer. I want to create my own artifacts for people to use & inhabit. I want to impress the world with: *Lampshades leaning like liquored bats, A ballet of oysters, The bowels of Kafka's hat, Backpacking love's rocky scree.* Y'unnerstand?

The story of Prometheus has never fully been told. He didn't remain tied to that rock nor did he die. The gods were not so lenient as to allow Prometheus the satisfaction of knowing his true punishment. Death was entirely too trivial & the gods were clever enough to recognize that blunt type of cockroach able to adapt to any situation given adequate time & regularity. The rock, the leather straps, the open wound, the exposed liver, the relentless eagle feasting on the ever-regenerating organ—all were mere preliminaries designed to whet the appetite, stir the creative juices. It was an exercise requiring little imagination & minimum effort. In fact, the whole process was completed in an instant by the simple action of a raised eyebrow. It is true that Prometheus suffered as no human could comprehend, but this feat only touched on the awesome powers of the gods & in no way reflected their truly malicious character, their base nature, their boundless capacity for spite & capriciousness. When it was obvious that Prometheus had grown insensitive or indifferent to the attacks, he was made to sleep, and, as the eagle* prepared to once more alight, the wound suddenly expanded & engorged the great bird.

When Prometheus awoke he was no longer bound, his wound had healed scarless & the eagle had disappeared. All evidence of Prometheus' ordeal had vanished without a trace & he was left with nothing but memories. To be sure, he trusted these memories, clung

* It should be mentioned that even the eagle by this time had become disenchanted with the game & had, in fact, developed a distaste for liver, approaching it with disgust, ripping it out unceremoniously, toying with it then dropping it into the valley to feed some other less discerning beast.

to them with a faith any saint would envy. But, over the centuries, he has discovered that memory is fallible, that History is manufactured, that most times what one wants to believe as true is far more convincing & pleasant than what is actually true, that dream & reality are not only two sides of the same coin, they are interchangeable & identical. Add to this passage of time certain vices: drugs, alcohol, sex, irregular eating habits, an obsession with the written word & it is no wonder that the past seems no more than a dream, a fiction, a bizarre fabrication contrived from a faulty brain.

This loss of memory, this mistrust, Prometheus blames on his vices & habits; his vices & habits he blames on the pain residing in his guts, a pain that varies in intensity & duration, sometimes dull & gripping, other times sharp & piercing. There is no activity not accompanied by pain. Even breathing is painful. Moreover, the pain increases during particular activities, activities that Prometheus finds unavoidable, inescapable as: attempting to remember, struggling to create, searching out the correct phrase, the exact word. The pain is experienced most unbearably precisely when he endeavours to reach out beyond his fingertips, outside his skin.

There are tricks to making us function as we should. I watched one mother sprinkle water on her child's back so that he'd pee in the toilet.

Donald Barthelme said, "Fragments are the only forms I trust." I agree. To complete something is to destroy it, to cut it off from any chance of growing, to limit interpretations. There is so much that is death around us & so many who practice the black art. Packagers. Tiers of loose ends. Finishers. Assassins. The term *abstract* sets their teeth on end. When Man Ray fills a urinal with flowers or Andy Warhol sets a tomato soup can on a pedestal & calls it ART, there is a run on ammo. One mustn't abstract a thing from its *normal* context & allow it to live apart. It mustn't be a fragment, a freak. It draws the curious from their shelters. It becomes too real. Almost holy. It disturbs the universe for a brief instant, until the hammer falls & the smoke clears & the dust settles & the hands are washed of blood. Then it's over. It's History. It fits.

I write letters to the editor to which, no reply, no print. The box remains empty the more often I look. There is a plague upon this earth. A plague upon me. The body is rejected. Even the placebos are spotted. I am wary. Weary of the tricks. Gutting to the feathers. PLAY ME OR TRADE ME, COACH! The uniform stiffens to the joints. I can't play ball.

I have cancer. No. No one has told me & I have not been to a doctor to confirm my diagnosis. MY DIAG-NOSIS. Notice, I do not say *suspicion*, for there can be no doubt to my mind: prolonged indigestion, lump in the throat, sore refusing to heal, change in mole, persist-ent cough, trouble swallowing—they have me & I them.

Is it possible to eliminate the obvious final effect in the face of so many causes? Can there indeed be no fire in the presence of so much smoke? I think not & remain resolute. There can be no doubt—I have cancer.

I have a spasm in my left eyelid. A muscle quivers & quakes like a ham actor performing death throes in Hamlet's last scene. We know he's gonna go at any time... (he's gotta go...) "Good night sweet prince, & flights of angels sing thee to thy rest"... In his own sweet time he's gonna go. We wait. The problem is, the eye also shudders, either as accomplice or in sympathy, & I don't know whether my eye will be content to simply

cease twitching along with his friend or attempt to upstage & carry out its act to the grave. "Ho! Horatio— let go the cup!"

It is difficult dealing with starry-eyed amateurs & over-zealous acolytes. Perhaps the eyeball will bow out & the eyelid will continue its comic gyrations indefinitely. Regardless, it is certain—I am not a well man &, while *the readiness is all*, I strain for the final curtain.

The library's a perfect place on a rainy day (reminds me of that line, *The grave's a fine & private place...* haha, oh well). Big change from sweeping floors & repairing toasters & fixing broken toilets. Nice to just wander through the shelves & explore; run my hands across the spines, flip through the pages, scribble down a few notes now & then. Maybe find some music worth taking home as well. Something different.

I would rather gutter with a barbarian than attempt your civilized tongue. What use is language beyond translation? Interpretation? Nothing clings to your words longer than shit to an asshole. They have been cleansed of any worthwhile meaning. Give me one worthwhile belch, a grunt, babble like a goddamn orang-utan—anything! But speak, fer Chrissakes, truly!

I watch with interest the young boy's careful disman-tling of the rose; the exactness with which he works in removing the petals, snapping each one at the base & pil-ing them off to the side. Reaching the centre, he cracks the seed pod like a nut & I read his disappointment at dis-covering no wires, no belts, no gears, no batteries to make the thing function. Also, the mechanism's total inability to snap back together. Completely useless, like one or two other boring toys he'd been given & scrapped almost immediately as being quite worthless & unamusing.

I continually fall in love with the wrong woman. Or the right woman but at the wrong time. Or the right time but the wrong woman. Or wrong woman, wrong time...

She never liked the way I massaged my fingers: stretching my hands, spreading the palms, extending the tips, then squeezing them together like a Chinese fan, each finger caressing the back of a previous finger then pressing the tips back into my palms so that, except for a red crescent in the centres, my nails turned completely white.

"Why do you do that?" she'd growl, in a tone reminiscent of my mother catching me one-on-one in a darkened corner of the shed. *Because it feels good* would not satisfy her just as *because it feels good* did not satisfy my mother. & there was no use joking! My simple act had varnished her face immune to laughter. Her mouth, nose & eyes were one-way mirrors, reflecting me, keeping me at bay like some wild animal. She looked like someone newly informed that what she had been eating was not food. I concealed my hands; hung them like meteorites in a deep-space orbit behind my back. She shook her head & that slight movement shattered me. I grunted, muttered a few sounds that were without meaning but were generally accepted as an admission or an apology.

Afraid to conjure up that mirror again, I carefully scrutinize all my behaviours, judge which are private, which public, prepare answers, consider probable responses, adjust replies, painfully list possible outcomes of every action & the actions of others, then proceed only with care, weighing my gains & losses against those around me. In order to maintain the status quo & achieve my fair share without expense to others, I fastidiously wipe my mouth, dab my chin, blow my nose, comb

my hair, tuck my shirt, pick my lint, straighten my tie, shine my shoes, hitch my pants & (only when I am quite certain that all backs are turned), address my crotch & resolutely pull up my fly.

&

You must believe me when I say that facts mean nothing to me anymore; that if I say that so-&-so said such-&-such or I mention a date, time or place & it is wrong or if I should misquote or mistake or misrepresent either on purpose or by accident it is not to confuse or mislead. It's just that, it simply doesn't matter—the original, naked truth. I am so full of information & ideas that it sloshes about inside me & assumes its own proper order & shape to suit its purpose. Question not the source but the intention & contrivance. That is, how does the info serve to illuminate & enhance the situation at hand?

Isn't it fascinating how the sounds of the day imperceptibly peel away toward evening so that some time around ten P.M. the tiny transistor radio which a few hours ago only peeped softly from the living room now presents itself a full-blown, charging mastadon trumpeting through the bedroom door.

Early morning tomorrow. Time to get some shut eye. Go pee, brush my teeth, drop my clothes on a chair, turn off the music, turn on the alarm & crawl between the sheets. I can barely make out the fragrance of perfume on the pillow beside me now, & the odour of sex has also nearly faded. I rub my eyes & roll onto my back, drawing the covers up to my chin.

Going out to a dinner party tonight. Should be fun. Haven't seen many of these folks for ages. Seems like we're never able to get together on our own anymore, we always need the excuse of a gathering. Doesn't seem to be just me either—the fact I'm getting more involved with a different crowd—everyone's busy; everyone has their own lives. At any rate, better pick up a jug of wine. A big jug.

1.

O.K. So travel the blue nightmare of your breath. See where it leads you. Into which bars, past which churches. Oh, don't get me wrong, I'm not saying you need God, it's just that, you need something to latch on to, something to keep your head above alcohol (it's a known fact you can't swim & you refuse to learn). I'm only telling you—we're all bored to tears with your boozy stink & we can no longer afford to bail you out of jail or pay your hospital bills (never mind apologizing to those you insult, repairing damages to property, making excuses to your boss, etc.). Understand, I'm not hitting you with this through lack of love but because of it. Make up your mind! & no bullshit about your writing. If you can't write without a drink beside you maybe you shouldn't be writing. At any rate, it's not your writing that's the problem (or maybe it is; in either case, it doesn't matter).

This door works two ways: it can lock you in or it can lock you out. Sure, you'll say that either way you're confined. Maybe that's true. But you can't continue to have it both ways. Not with me. You've got exactly sixty seconds—choose your trap.

2.

When asked in an interview, "What is jazz?" Louis Armstrong replied, "If you don't know, Ah cain't nevah tell ya." When asked, "Why do you drink?" I quote Louis Armstrong.

3.

There are things that frighten me. Like, the bottom of a glass. Friends & bartenders know this & are quick to replenish, stopping only when I am blind-drunk or passed out on the floor. It's not that I'm an alcoholic, you understand. It's just that I'm so afraid of emptiness, whatever I do, I do in excess.

4.

I could offer some other reasons such as:
i) sometimes it is precisely at those moments when I am blind-drunkest that I see most clearly, or,
ii) alcohol strips away social veneers or reveals more interesting ones, or,
iii) alcohol allows me to put up with certain situations, certain people I would prefer to avoid, or,
iv) alcohol alters perceptions in new & exciting ways, or,

v) alcohol helps me to escape problems, avoid making decisions, or,

vi) alcohol stirs the artist in me, or,

vii) I drink because I despise perfection & order.

As you can probably imagine, these reasons are normally met with various degrees of disbelief, skepticism, disdain or ridicule, which is why I prefer to quote Louis Armstrong. There is one other reason for avoiding explanations:

5.

A major sign of alcoholism is that a person tends to offer explanations for their drinking habits. I also never admit that I should go on the wagon for a while, since: *a second major sign of alcoholism is that a person tends to admit needing to "lay off the sauce for a spell."*

6.

I stagger into a bar. Before, knew everyone. Now? Nothing familiar: music, decor, faces—even the smoke hangs differently—heavy, heavy, heavy; everything weighing against me, collapsing strange & awkward. Been years, I know. & yet... sure, nothing repeats & you can't go back & the waitress calls me *sir* like any other stranger, but still...I drink & I think, *there must be a way.* All I need is an entrance. A little introduction. The right combination of this-&-that, like: ice tinkling a glass, the burn of whiskey, the elevation of a hand to a certain height, the wrinkle of a nose, the twist of a lip, the angle of an eyebrow, the pointing of a finger in some

particular fashion; gestures settling into place, taking their positions like characters in an old familiar movie. One more drink &, "ROLL FILM"—it's happening, happening—&, "Excuse me, miss. Remember me?" Her face tilts into the frame. "Remember you?" The images merge, &, "Why, sure. Sure! 'Course I remember you. Who you tryin' to kid?" & now she's smiling, & the drinks keep coming, & the film keeps rolling without a flutter, without a break.

I don't believe it. All I've done this weekend is sit around the apartment with my finger up my ass, watching TV, playing solitaire & basically fucking the dog.

But then, it doesn't matter what I do. Whether I do anything or nothing at all. Unlike Space, which leaves me uncomfortable & ill-fitting, Time passes without a care or thought as to my well-being. It brands me with its mark & I am denied the barest glimpse.

The mind should not be allowed to wander freely. The territory is too vast. Nothing good can come of it. Except death. A relative good, granted. But to be lost forever? Trapped in some godforsaken pit? Pursued by vicious animals? Fear offers limited protection & adventure; offers limited solace. Infinitely worse is the stark loneliness. Bushed, they call it. When the senses give way to the barkish moon. Coyotes howl at the edge of

the clearing. It is only my constant fire keeps them at bay. It becomes increasingly difficult. There is so little here that burns.

As I open the door the entire landscape slips past me, drawn into the house as easily as water drawn up a straw. Facing out, space stretches its star-riddled body across the doorframe & infinitely back, allowing the illusion of seeming both very near &, at the same time, very distant. There is no horizon, no landmark, no means of measuring distance, position or time. There is only space; only the dull phosphorescence of what may or may not be stars. Facing in, nature has already begun arranging itself neatly, orderly, either by stacking on shelves, nestling comfortably in cupboards or by curling warm & snug into cushions, chairs & carpets.

The door is trembling. The door demands closure. I stand, my eyes study the two sides of the door, fix on the glass-handle doorknobs. My hand passes, first to one handle, then the other; touching, caressing, still not gripping, as though expecting a hint: a gentle movement, a sudden warmth.

I am single, a bachelor, & *How wonderful*, I think, *to be free & unencumbered, without a mate or family to worry about, to tie me down; to be able to come & go as I please at any hour of the day or night; to see whomever I please.* But this thought disappears by the time I reach the door, for a family man *must* open the door, *must* venture out to his job, *must* run errands, *must* return home, *must* make enquiries of his wife & children. He is able to act without thinking of this-or-that-other-thing & so his days are rich, full & useful. I, on the other hand, am not compelled to any action. Least of all opening this door, leaving my room, entering the confident, bustling world of family men. The door is proof of this. It shrugs its shoulders & scolds me, "Where do you intend to go & why? That outside world is not meant for you. It's much too big. You'd be lost out there, unable to function. Better that you remain here, in this room, which is more your size. Better yet, why not crawl back to your bedroom which is still too large. Half a room, a corner is all you really require. You are small, have narrow shoulders & almost no depth. Hunch in your chair like a clam, ink yourself to a square of white paper, fold like a letter & discover your freedom buried in a deep womb of brown manila."

I hardly begin & it changes. Not in the sense that writing alters thought. I mean FORMALLY, it changes. Becomes alien. There are ghosts in me. I know. Maybe *ghosts* is wrong. Presences. I don't believe in ghosts. The normal sense. Presences is better. Presences with a will to affect me. I AM NOT A BIG THINKER. I DO NOT PRETEND TO BE. THESE WORKS ARE NOT MINE. Then whose? IF I knew. If I knew, then...? If I knew, then...what?

Catch myself staring vacantly at a broken doorknob on my desk. Don't know how long I've been staring. Nothing special about it. The doorknob. I found it on the ground one day & slipped it into my bag. It's made of smooth, polished chrome. The metal connecting rod is snapped at the end. I pick it up. It's cool to the touch. I see my reflection alter as I turn the knob with my hand.

D.H. Lawrence preached in his works that homosexuality & promiscuity were the basis of the downfall of civilization. Yes. *Lady Chatterley's Lover* is a moralistic novel. Beyond the seemingly gratuitous fucking in the beginning, it is love which allows Lady Chatterly to orgasm & it is the ideal of love which makes it possible for her & the gamekeeper to transcend their animalistic cravings & enter the realm of platonic bliss during their separation. For Lawrence, *man* is in opposition to *nature* & the struggle is toward purity. This was his fiction. His life, conversely, was one of weakness & debauchery, he having had an estimated five hundred lovers of either sex. Lawrence used his art as a confession box where he played the roles of sinner & priest. For what reasons? Why rebel against his experience of the world? In the face of so much contrary evidence, why not change philosophies? Ingrained, puritanical guilt stemming from a strict, religious background, possibly. The inability to reconcile how one feels with how one is supposed to feel. The desire to teach the world to be better than he could be himself. Did he consider himself the suffering Christ sent to redeem us at the cost of his own tubercular life? Preaching from the gutter of experience & drowning in his own black blood. Was it a game? A bit of sex plus a bit of morality equals lots of controversy & a lot more readers? Or was he simply another poor, son of a bitch human being who felt he'd been dealt a bad hand from a crooked deck? Beaten before he started. Nature was not a nemesis but an undertaker. Lawrence knew he couldn't keep his body so he intended to use it up & shuck it IN HIS OWN WAY. If anything lived past the flesh it had to be his soul or his art & these rubbed together like two

cats in heat, sparks issuing from their fur. Lawrence blazed. It was enough & this is my story.

My passion is not perfect. It waits in dark corners, behind shrubbery, between cracks in walls & curtains. It stands at the bottom of stairs & escalators seizing at ankles, surveying knees, contemplating lines formed between flesh & clothing: thighs, hips, backs, breasts. A lengthy climb reveals the fringed hem of delicate slip or, more rarely, the tops of gartered nylon.

When I approach a door, my eye trembles in its socket, struggles to free itself, press its body against the keyhole. At a theatre I am drawn to sit behind a woman whose long hair hangs over the back of her seat. As the evening progresses, my hand inches forward, along my thigh, across my knee. The tips of my fingers are pushed by the palm, the palm by the wrist until the entire hand floats off the knee, drifts like a kite, the string playing out slowly, slowly, the fingers unbending, stretching—I can hear them move, the tiny bones, shifting in their joints.

If her head leans back now, even slightly, her hair will touch my hand. If my shoulder leans forward now, even slightly, my hand will be buried in her hair; stroking, gripping, disturbing the stillness, scattering the light. Her cheek tilts & my hand retreats; pulls back as though scorched, as though discovered. Her ear searches for a word, a kiss. My eyes scan the theatre, feet cross, knees lock, hands dive for cover. She laughs &, in one swift motion tosses back her hair, returning it draped behind her seat. Already, my hands have escaped the weight of my legs & are manoeuvring down my thighs, fingertips dragging my entire body toward the precipice of knees. As the edge nears, there is the feeling that once my

hands lift off, there will be nothing—neither weight, nor height, nor ceiling to prevent me from shooting off into space, toward the centre of some burning star & certain annihilation.

Women love the truth. They languish in it. They sport it like a war wound. A brand. A mirror that reflects stone. They play Phoenix rising, while men peck the cold ashes.

"Did you fuck him?"

"Do you want me to tell you?"

"No."

"Did you fuck her?"

"Do you want me to tell you?"

"Yes."

"You do? Now?"

"Now."

"While we're making love?"

"While we're fucking. Tell me. Tell me everything. Why you did it & how you did it. Give me the details."

"You want to be buried in shit."

"No. I want to be cleansed of shit. Why don't you say something? Has your tongue turned to marble? Are you a statue? Speak to me. Speak... Speak..."

I'm at the bar & there's a couple seated a stool away from me. They're having this low boil discussion over a few drinks. She's accusing him of staring at some woman on the street earlier. He says that he wasn't looking at her, he was looking at her car. The discussion goes on like this. I recall seeing a commercial to the same affect & the guy actually *was* looking at the car. I don't recall what make the car was, I was looking at the woman. The couple next to me keep at it, the woman finally saying, "Why can't you just be honest with me? I can accept anything as long as it's honest." The guy doesn't know what to say.

It really is a monster. A 1930 Bugatti 41 Royale. Beautiful. With its one hundred & sixty-nine inch wheelbase, the sleek beast straddles two white lines & catches the admiration of a pair of parking meters. Not a mark or scratch anywhere. Spotless. Polished chrome fender, headlamps, grill—even the hood ornament—a chrome elephant reared up on its hind legs bellowing, CHARGE! Right out of the past & still kicking.

The body itself is painted ice-cream white, topped with a black convertible roof. The front wheel wells arc the massive twenty-four inch wheels & slope gently back to become running boards. The trunk is also black & attached to the rear bumper, the spare tire hunches like

a blocker for the Chicago Bears.

Through the window, the interior of the Bugatti sparkles plush & roomy with real leather upholstery, wood grain dash & heavy-duty rubber flooring. Lying on the front seat is a pair of fur-lined gloves, a white silk scarf, a carved walking stick with ebony handle, & a black umbrella. Unfolded across the back seat is a newspaper. The headline reads: AMELIA EARHART SOLOS ACROSS ATLANTIC, dated May 21, 1932. On the street side of the car stands a man half in, half out, one foot on the floor, one arm leaning against the open door. He's wearing a grey suit, spats & (even with the sun shining down) rubbers & a black overcoat. He surveys the scene with seemingly detached interest, like one of those mobsters you see in the old black-&-whites, casing the joint before the big heist. With his free hand, he pushes back his hat, sniffs the air & smiles as if having made a discovery, like: the rain has stopped & the sun is out.

On a day like today, what does it matter that he's dressed for the wrong weather & the Bugatti's top is up? On a day like today, what does it matter that the man is dead & buried over fifty years & the Bugatti is quietly rotting in a junk yard somewhere in the history of Chicago?

72

Just another one of those days. I sit at the desk, seemingly drained of life's blood or every other vital fluid, assessing my situation & wondering what's to be done.

Yes! Pay my debts & get the hell out of here! "Flee on your donkey!" said Sexton. "Anywhere! Anywhere out of this world!" cried Baudelaire. Voices from the Grand Hotel. Asylums for unravelled brains. Put distance between me & my impending history: accidents, hospitalizations, amputations, death of friends & family, my mother's dance with blindness. I'm tired with the role of *rock*. This Bakoo is stuffed! I can't eat another sin. I can't write another epitaph! The world grows old & sick around me. I can face my pain but I can't face theirs. I'll respond to each new tragedy with tears. The nightmares will be as fierce but, to not have to be there, to not have to face it & then continue on my own seems the far better route.

The guilt I can handle. It's the eternal helplessness that kills.

On a sand dune in the middle of the desert, a large wooden ship rocks uneasily under the influence of whirling winds. The sails have been shredded by the effects of sand. Canvas fragments twist about the mast or flap from broken spars. The hull also suffers, portions having been torn away, the rest scarred & pitted.

Two men on camels face each other, face the ship. "How?" "How?" The questions escape the perfect roundness of the lips, flutter like a bird toward the ship. The ship, embarrassed, bows forward, allows the sand to cover it like a wave.

Makers of rooms. Builders of walls & dividers. We gear for separation. A room for guests. A room to cook. A room to sleep & sex. A room to eliminate. A room for you & a room for me. A final room to free baby from rude sounds, harsh words &... love.

There is a person balanced on ledge. Wait! Cancel that. I have forgotten to formulate a ledge. For a person to balance on a ledge there must first be a ledge. It makes sense. People are not cartoon characters. They need something solid. I therefore create a ledge for this purpose. The purpose of supporting my person. It has no other function which makes detailing it unimportant. Whatever happens next will depend entirely on the strength of my ledge. We will have to wait & see. We will have to keep an eye on it to discern how it stands up under pressure. The ledge may be unimportant in itself but it bears our attention.

The person (meanwhile) has disappeared. Vanished without a trace.

Where is the ledge?

I'd like to write a series of, say, forty poems based on paintings by Magritte. I'd use the titles of the paintings, but the poems must not be mere descriptions. In fact, the poems should have little to do with the paintings as far as representation is concerned. In this way, the poems may be written first & the titles jumbled & pinned on randomly later. Thus, the poems would exist more apart from the paintings. The process would be more akin to musical interpretations or variations on certain themes, events & objects; as Mussorgsky's *Pictures at an Exhibition*. Upon reading the poems someone should say, "They remind me of Magritte. They have that kind of *feel* about them. I don't know what it is, but I feel it."

& the room with its. Square. No balcony. A window, only, to raise & stick one's head. Lean through &. Sniff. The air. Ponderous. Thick. The exhaust of liquid dinosaurs &. A door, also. Leading to a hallway but not out. Never out. Circling back again to the same & returning. The same. Unchanging, back-again-back-again-jiggedy-jig & returning the same. Unbroken. The same circle in. The same square. Room with floor, walls, ceiling, window & a door. One lock keeps the honest people (who are the worst anyway). Keeps them. Circling. This/their room. The same. With (& we go around again): floor, walls, ceiling, window & a door.

One lock &. No balcony. To sit. To sun. To leap from. The room, only. With its circle/square. Pattern. Devouring itself & its (one more round gentlemen, please, &, taking stock): floor, walls, ceiling, window & a door. Also, one lock—open—&. Circling. The square.

She just called. She says she's coming over. She says she needs to see me. That could mean anything. I crack a bottle of wine & pour a glass. *Anything.*

There is a conveyor belt & on either side a row of workers construct some kind of complicated machine or instrument, piece by piece. These workers are dressed in similar uniforms of a nondescript nature making it impossible to tell which are male, which female. It doesn't matter. Such definition would in no way affect the chore at hand. They repeat their specific functions & there are no stalls, no hesitations. Whatever it is they are building gathers its own definite form in its own required time.

No one on the assembly line has any idea what the

device is or what it does or how it operates. No one knows what it looks like when completed. Even the last people on the line are ignorant since it travels around a corner & disappears into another room.

As a change, the workers switch positions periodically, enabling them to attach a different piece of equipment. In this way, everyone knows as much as the other about the construction of the device; everyone is equal. No one goes into the other room. There is no need. The same sounds emanate from the other room as are produced in this room. One assumes the same work. The workers of this room do not converse with the workers of the other room. There are separate dining halls, separate washrooms. At the end of shift, they leave by different exits.

Outside of these walls no one discusses occupations. They claim there is no need. This is partly true. After all, since one worker is the same as an other, what is there to discuss? What could there be? Yet, while none would admit it, there is some fear. A superstition. A silly story that hangs about the air & tells us that, long ago (& the factory has been around since before anyone can remember), a worker crossed into the other room, staggered back at the sight, went mad & died with the release of a single, ear-splitting scream. Oh, they are not afraid of the worker's ghost, or of the wind that howls constantly through cracks in walls & windows. That would make their case at least respectable, almost admirable. No. Their fear takes the form of a phobia. It is completely irrational & has absolutely no basis in fact. The fear is this: the workers believe that while the device is being constructed in one room, it is being dismantled in the

other. *Ad infinitum.* A ridiculous notion not worth considering. Still, the fear is real. Still, no one investigates.

Time for discovery has expired. No need to remove my head from the oven, I've exchanged conversation with gas for too long. My brain is vapour & my voice remains shackled to the grill. Also...don't be alarmed by my blank gaze (I was never really here, pasted to my face, anyway), the best of me was always poems ricocheting from enamel or trapped-racing through metal piping waiting for some human heat to set me off. But that's changed. Now I've become practical; a functional. I will float like the holy Hindenburg, seek out my moment of tangible lightning, explode, burn & cast my lot indelibly in the sacred ink of newsprint.

"He provided quite a blast," they'll say. "Illuminated the heavens—& what warmth! Who'd've thought he had it in him?"

Meanwhile, this stove shall take my place. Note the resemblance: dull finish, wrinkled, glassy eyed, heavy headed, tired nose, nervous lips, sunken cheeks—even my characteristic shoulder sag! *Too much of words hast thou, poor stove!* Poetry drags you screeching earthward like a pilotless bat while I drift lightly up, up & up— silent—toward the clouds.

On the beach, a tipped sand pail. A shovel rests on

the spilled contents: rocks, shells, sand. This picture was not planned. It occurred. One simple, random action & the universe seems out of joint.

"*Seems*, mother? I know not *seems*."

Water seeks its own level. Order dons its inky cloak & assumes. *Assumes*. The world clippety-clops along like a nag with blinders. Unerring purpose. The pail tips & the contents spill to form a new pattern. The true harmony is chaos.

They've got me cleaning the grease trap in the kitchen. *Low man on the totem pole*. They say it probably hasn't been touched since the hotel opened. By the look of it, I think they're right. I'll be surprised if I don't find a few fatty carcasses while I'm at it. Nothing too complicated about the job, just open the trap, reach inside & scoop out the shit. I expect it'll keep me busy most of the day. If not, I'll be sure to make it stretch. Hell, it's enough work for one day, for any one guy.

There are no jobs for unspecific geniuses or people of broad talents. No room at the inn for Renaissance persons. They are labelled unfocussed. Jack of all trades & master of none. Merely egocentric. We are raised to pursue a single goal, a single career along a ready-made path. There is room for alternative but not deviation. Deviation results in banishment from the normal world & there is no returning. One is branded; headed off to Nod.

I'm intelligent & well mannered enough to get into sales or management. I'm physically able to dig a hole or pave a road. But the brand inevitably shows through the veneer. I am recognized & these employers of people realize I do not fit their thirty-year plan. I will likely not last six months. Bored, I will sail off in search of grapefruit-sized diamonds & golden fleeces. Worse, I will draw much of the staff with me. At least, as far as the door.

When I look in the mirror, I see nothing unusual & it seems damned difficult not to fit when so many parts align. Yet, I manage. I manage. People of awkward genius. Of discomfiting talents.

After giving a reading of my poetry at a local art gallery, an elderly woman approached me & proceeded to use her heavy German accent as a cannon to launch her verbal assault upon my person.

"Young man, I listened to your reading & I must say I find you rude, crude, vulgar, base, profane, egotistical & loud. You say whatever you want & don't give a damn about anyone else."

I was about to reply, though I don't know what I would've said to her. I do remember that I felt genuinely touched by her response. I had reached someone. She continued with a smile,

"& I want you to know that I loved your reading immensely. It was very refreshing. Now, I will buy your book. That is what is done, yes?"

I had copies of a self-published chapbook. "Yes," I said. "Sometimes. I feel as though I should give it to you."

"Nonsense. Did the books print themselves for free? I will pay."

I took the money from her & we talked for a few more minutes. She had arrived with a friend, out of curiosity. She didn't know much about poetry (as the saying goes) but she knew what she liked. She liked me.

& if Jesus hadn't died on the cross, had instead been found innocent; pardoned & released; declared a free man able to preach & believe anything he wished, would this turnabout have invigorated him, caused him to increase his teachings, improve his effectiveness, apply himself more fully to spreading the word of God? Or was this to be his grand finale, his trump card suddenly snatched out from under him? How hard had he worked toward implementing his own crucifixion & how much depended upon it?

His followers have already begun planning for the funeral: the coffin built, the burial site named, invitations sent, the food ordered. Lives are being shaped & altered, new leaders are being chosen. Ways are being devised which will enable others to continue with the work as a consequence of Jesus' death. These are not events easily tampered with by men or by gods. For all the good Jesus had done, for all the miracles he had performed, for all the times he had been correct, a crowd needs only one mistake, one missed trick to turn & shout, "Liar! Fraud! Fake!"

When will they perform their final base hysterectomy & leave me hollow as a doorknob? Their preference is usable empty vessels & I am full of myself. Like a stone is full of a stone; diamond of diamond. They are sore afeared!! I refuse to be drained then filled with them or any other mud. Still, they are creatures of habit & trust the old ways. The knife then, doctor! Cut deeply & painfully. Scoop this baby-bag clear through to the rind. I will not surprise you with butterflies, tarantulas or pre-historic lizards (though I wish I could). Nothing but flesh & blood. Nothing to me but me to the last cell.

Dear editor:
Once again I have exercised my right not to vote. Surprise—although derided, I was not struck dead by vagrant lightning nor was the country spiralled into the abyss. We are all here & nothing has changed. How could it when choice is narrowed to one money manager over another? Mirror images of the same thin shadow. When was it ordained that accountants were created to assume the position: to run a business, to run a country? Where are the hunters, the healers, the artists, the philosophers? I would prefer a lunatic in office shedding tears of blood, wailing & moaning in real anguish for the people & their plight to a politician delivering monologues of squares & zeros.

Offer me a dim-witted,wart-nosed hunchback with
no tongue & halitosis; one who throws its hands into
the air at the problems of equality, freedom & mere
subsistence; a hunchback who concentrates on *how* to
live. Eye to eye with the impossible, laughing full-out
from the belly & dancing a jig in the jaws of a snark.
Not admitting defeat but realizing it is time we stud-
ied causes rather than effects. Offer me that & I'll
vote for the hunchback everytime.

Even wearing clothes, I'm naked. My eyes betray my
genitals & no one stops to stare. They look away, embarrassed. For me? No need. I am Peter Pan with a penis in
search of Never-never land.

André Gide wrote in *The Immoralist*, "I believe any extreme sensitivity may become the cause of pleasure or of pain depending on whether the organism is robust or sickly. All that disturbed me once has become delicious to me."

The problem, as I see it, is that the human organism is entirely too sickly today. Or too dull. In the main, humans are not much sensitive to either pleasure or pain. They waffle about in some nether region of sentimentality, insulated by their possessions. There is no need & no desire to go out beyond their comfort zone, outside of themselves. These human organisms are fast becoming self-contained, self-sufficient & self-gratifying. Classic examples of Leibnitz's windowless Monads.

My heros have always been tragic figures. Hamlet drowned. Rimbaud drowned. Van Gogh drowned. Marilyn Monroe drowned. Anne Sexton drowned. Sylvia Plath drowned. John Berryman drowned. Richard Brautigan drowned. Not the real drowning but the *real* drowning. The drowning that has occurred long before the gas or the pills take effect or the bullet penetrates the skin. It doesn't matter what's written on the coroner's report. This death is secondary. A technicality necessary to clean up the books. Each face stared up from the bottom of a pool. As in Stevie Smith's poem, "Not Waving

But Drowning," these folks paddled, *Much too far out all [their] lives.*

Virginia Woolf sought water when the knives failed. Before stepping in she filled her pockets with stones. This is not the action of an irrational person, but a thorough one. Jack Spicer claimed that language did him in, while those that knew him blamed the booze. At any rate, no amount of Kleenex could dry his tears. Death by drowning. Tennessee Williams choked on the plastic cap from a pill bottle. What was it doing in his mouth? Even the simplest chores are impossible in a world filled with so much water. Death by drowning. The arm-waving that resulted in so many false rescues was not a plea for salvation. They were giving up the ghosts that haunted them. Death by drowning. All my heroes dead or dying, drowned or drowning.

I know my visit is not planned. Certainly I have no reason to be here nor does my friend expect me. Rather, he stands at the door in his crisp suit & remains quite speechless at the sight of me. I say hello, he crouches, waving me in with his thin right hand while attempting to block, with his left, some object which rests behind his heels—a box—long & narrow, approximately two feet by two feet by six feet. (I refrain from using the image *coffin-like* as it would only excite my writer's imag-

ination & have me suspiciously questioning or fantasizing over my friend's behaviour—my best friend, I might add—who must have his reasons for not confiding in me). As he says nothing, I make my way into the living room. He follows at a short distance, we both sit & merely stare at each other for a few minutes. "Brandy?" he stammers, breaking the silence. "Fine," I say, & as he raises the bottle I notice it is empty. "Oh, I'm sorry," he points. "I'm so sorry." & he cries. Great tears fill his eyes & dampen his cheeks. He shakes his head, all the while pointing & staring at the empty bottle. "I am so sorry." We both fidget. "Don't worry. It's all right. Really it is. I only dropped by to say hello. You couldn't have known." "Is it all right? Is it really?" "Of course," I say. "Besides, I should leave now anyway. It's time." I rise, walk to the end of the hallway & stop at the door. I look down. The box is gone. I open the door & enter the dark night. The door closes & I am unable to move. Enclosed in blackness, I am lying flat on my back, my hands folded across my chest. There is the sound of a hammer & the squeak of metal nails penetrating wood. I bolt upright & discover myself standing at the end of the hallway. I am crying & in my sweating hands is an empty brandy bottle. Further down the hall a door closes & on the floor rests a coffin. "I'm sorry," I weep. "I'm so sorry."

& in the slappy, wrungedover mourning Johhny-pants whopped up a breakfast of thunderful womblettes, bashed round pertaters, wampagne with ojay, frish blued joe & ghosted ruffians smooched in jamberry. We was extramerous in our mystery. Our bods rubbled & the noggins spook harsh ka-banggggg! reverbs like reveille-on-an-anvil, grungy tonguesters & floopy tums. Offers us a bit of *air-orf-the-dawg* in the warm shapes of brewskies. Land two ass burns & a case of the fivvering shits.

The day, she begins.

Oh, man—what a weird couple of weeks. It's not like I've really *been* anywhere, yet I come back & every-thing's as it was. Aren't there any unemployed writing fairies or writing elves out there? Hasn't this pencil known me long enough to keep going without me? I mean, I don't even know where to begin. I don't even know how.

We need new words, new phrases for lovers, like, "I snubbled in & bopped her wimpy." She bartled, "Berrypie me sugarnose." I did. She kissed my pottle. I toddled her gymrack. We cooched. Smak, smak. Glub, glub. Our patters yin-yanged. "Folly soak! Morph me jigger pod!" we sang. Our flimish rimmed to gnashing, "Lubber suck! Pitter-pat! Nurl me tonnees!" I nurdled her tonnees & bit her graflit. "Ahhhhhhh!" she plied & waled her fleshies off my toff. "Ipsy noodle bunny chop. Ipsy warble. Ipsy lapso. Ipso facto." I gleaned her miff, mewing lun-lun on me oomlah & gooshed. "OWWWooooohhhaahhhhhhh, ah, ah... ah...ah...ah..." we turtled & jagged, slivving & rimming. "...ah... ah... mmmmmmmmmmmm" we moogled. "Glub, glub honey-beard." "Glub, glub liquor-stick." Morning melded & we drippled op to gleep.

During a storm she'd position herself spread-eagled & naked from the waist down in front of the fireplace, & masturbate. She believed the old tale that lightning enters a house through the chimney & leaves out the window. One hand sparked the tiny bud, while the other guided the plastic Virgin Mary up her vagina.

"Holy Mary, mother of God..." she murmured.

She prayed to the storm, to the restless sky to deliver that fatal shock, that bolt of pure, electric heat.

1.

I want my words to strike like an arrow which, unwaver-
ing, passes through the body. There is then, the telling
impact of the stone head, the questioning look as one
attempts to discover the cause & the trickle of red which
remains to indicate that an event has occurred.

2.

Words that must necessarily assume an order, but tenta-
tive, threaten to blow apart at any given moment. A
story like a peacock with nitro-trembling bones & you
are trapped, watching, waiting for any nervous twitch,
any abrupt itch: the flap of a wing, the blink of an eye.

3.

I'm struggling with words. Can you believe it?! Like
they're flesh & blood or something. I should be so
lucky—to grab some word around its scrawny little neck
&... squeeze.

4.

It's only my contempt for words that keeps me writing.
How be serious over a handful of lofty balloons that
explode under the prick of a sharp eye? Gloss & sparkle!
They are the paint of poets & have nothing to do with
Truth, Duty, Beauty, even Reality! Chimeras. They do
not explain-away the world. They do not eliminate war.
They do not drag the worm-torn body of a dead brother
alive & handsome from the grave. Worthless! Worthless
these words. Worthless all the words in all the languages!

I am the voice inside the box. Why? Because I have the unenviable task of relating information best suited for a mechanical device. I am soul-less & lack all pride & modesty. We are accustomed to hearing such information from machines or from voices that resemble machines. "Three jillion people suicided today by hacking themselves to pieces with shards of designer sunglasses. The weather remains clear & hot." If such jargon were entrusted to real people we would all cringe with embarrassment. We would stand up & leave.

He was afraid of his body. Didn't like the way it acted on its own, contrary to his mind; always reaching out & grabbing, always gathering material goods, always interfering with his quest for spiritual enlightenment, always blocking the road to salvation. What could he do? His body was insatiable. It had strong physical desires which in no way could be deterred or altered & which constantly proved rude & embarrassing: eating, drinking, smoking, fornicating, defecating; making wheezing, snoring, growling, gurgling, farting sounds; & dragging him into places he couldn't take his mother. Imagine the happiness he would discover if not for his body! Imagine how the gods would smile upon him, bless him! Imagine his eternal joy if only...yes! That's it! Cast off the unholy thing! Unburden himself!

"If thine ear offends thee..." He ruptures both eardrums with a pointed stick.

"If thine nose..." He axes his nose.

"If thine tongue..." He slices his tongue at the root.

"If thine teeth..." He smashes out his teeth.

"If thine legs..." He chainsaws his legs.

"If thine testicles..." He crushes them between two stones.

"If thine anus..." He mortars his anus.

"If thine arms..." He guillotines his arms.

Sitting straight-backed on the ground, he grins like an amputated Buddha & meditates toward heaven. While he prays, a thief relieves him of his wallet & slits his throat. He dies guttering like a doused candle.

Then there's the one who rages out of doors & screams at the top of his lungs for the snow to stop falling. Everyone thinks he's crazy. "Stop! Stop for Chrissakes! Enough fucking snow already!" No backflip allusion to that bearded King Canute who tried to test his connection with God by ordering the tide to retreat. No, this fellow is not a King or a priest or even a dog catcher. He is berserk. He is mad. Worse, he is a nuisance to everyone around him. But, what a feeling! To suck the lungs full of frozen air & spit it back as steam; to challenge the elements for a moment, at least; to bare the

pagan soul & exercise oneself as a participant in the natural order, as a power to be recognized & reckoned with.

A moment of utter selfishness, utter life.

&

There is a snowstorm out there, but I'm not budging. I'm hanging inside where it's warm & toasty. I've got a glass of brandy, a bowl full of mixed nuts, Bach on the stereo & I'm wrapping Christmas presents. If the telephone rings, I'm screening my calls. Right now, the snow looks fabulous whipping against the window & clinging to the trees. Like the proverbial Winter Wonderland. If there's six feet of it waiting for me outside in the morning, I'll deal with it then. For now, "Let it snow, let it. snow, let it snow..."

The one who asked *what's the joke?* & we tried to invent one or make some sense out of the statement *what's the joke? what's the joke?* he kept askin' & no one knew what the fucking joke was & it pissed us off 'cause who the hell was he some smartass acting prof from New York & so what was it some kind of game or head game or was he king shit of turd island or was he rubbin' our noses in it & *what's the joke? what's the joke?* & what's it got to do with the price of shit in China all right no one's gettin' off on this joke trip except him who's laughin' his fat ass off while we're the dumb fuckers payin' for all this shit & maybe that's the joke & we tell him & he says *what's the joke? what's the joke?* so we haven't got it & we haven't got it & we don't want to think about it & all the time we are thinkin' about it & if he's tryin' to pull a fast one then it's workin' but what's it got to do with actin' we ask & he says *what's the joke?* like we expected & we say how do we know *what's the joke* if you don't tell us? & he smiles like a cunt & says (you know what he says 'cause it's like a broken record by now) *what's the joke?* & the prick laughs behind his beard & you want to smack him but you don't 'cause you know deep down there's somethin' funny not quite right no one wants to admit defeat 'cause that's what smackin' him would be or maybe that's what he's after a gut response as we're stewin' in our own sweat he says *what's the joke?* we explode there is no joke there is no joke you bastard & we stare at him & he laughs & says that's it that's the joke & we're catchin' flies & our assholes are wound up like clocks & he's laughin' & we've got it like Zen only different 'cause the joke is that there is no joke & that's funny man, the realization that you can burn your ass all

your life lookin' for the joke & it ain't *there* out there
that the joy & the laughter is in you all the time & you
just have to open yourself up to it & let it roll out any
old time you want & that had us rollin' in the aisles man,
that simple thing had us rollin' & it was a trip & it was
a blast & it had somethin' to do with theatre.

&

Most of today's theatre is a corpse being carried on
the back of an idiot. It is difficult, almost impossible, to
tell where the one begins & the other ends.

I do not phone. I am unable. They must phone me. They must need me. They must want to talk. They are lonely. They are desperate. They are bored. They are horny. They are in love. They want love. I do not phone. I am unable. Unallowed. They are married. They are secure. They are afraid. They are far away. I despise the distance of phones. The mechanics. They must be within reach. I am not comforted by the call. It is an easy thing. To call. For them. Necessary for a time. Talk as a substitute for actions. We fill the space with sounds. We hang up. We return to our lies. Our emptinesses.

You know... I just get into it, just get into it & it's time to stop. Time to sleep or time to go to work. Why? Because one requires sleep; because one has bills to pay so one needs money so one works at a job that feeds as it kills. Meanwhile, one is in awe of those earlier novelists tramping though the sewers of Paris discussing Art & Philosophy, begging glasses of wine, stumbling into the arms of beautiful, passionate lovers & generally fucking the system. Only later does one begin to question: who pays the rent, does the laundry, buys the groceries; how come no ugly, boring lovers, no disease; where does the money come from to pay for paper, pens, pencils, erasers, typewriters, envelopes when I can barely afford postage? Paid for by patrons, institutions, relatives & even savings accounts. Bastards! They could afford a life of poverty.

Tonight it is true—I shall accomplish nothing. But then, what is there to accomplish? Even at the end there will only be these few silly words, so what will it matter, a few more or a few less? What will it matter if the light goes out now or a few hours from now or a few years from now? All that matters (& this is the one great sad fact) is that the light will go out, either on its own or by my deliberate hand.

Piss, fuck & shit! I've been laid off. When they told me, I went for a few drinks after work & ended up around midnight in the middle of an empty parking lot, the snow falling all around me, bawling my eyes out. Now it's been another three days & I sit here thinking, what am I supposed to do? I'm strapped as it is, how am I going to survive on UI? Plus, it takes forever to get. They say it may only last a few weeks. Then again, it might take til Spring, when business picks up. I should get out. I should go for a walk. I should go & be with someone. I know it does no good staying in my apartment. & looking at my writing just drives me crazier. But I also know that I'm not good company at this point. Besides, the snow continues to rage & it's freezing out there. So, I lie here staring at the ceiling, feeling sorry for myself.

You leave your mark like a dog. You needn't piss, just touch, & the stench lingers like a scar.

Boundaries are never clear, like dreams or memories, but even a wisp of you, a breath, a hint, & people, places go unheard, unnoticed, ignored—like graveyards or the tears of aging whores.

Unable to stand it any longer I go to a phone booth & dial my number. I listen to it ring & imagine I'm at home listening to it ring. That's nice, I think. A caller. Someone wanting to talk to me, needing me. A relative perhaps. A friend. A lover. I let it ring. I am unavailable. I am wrestling with the muse & cannot be disturbed. I let it ring. Whoever is calling must be patient, must understand my need for solitude. I let it ring until I am embraced with warmth. The muse is tenacious. I let it ring. I smile. I hang up.

There is nothing unusual. A cockroach crawls across my tongue. I lock the beast behind my teeth until it resumes its legless pink. Bells ring before the clap. Lights glow before the tickle of electricity. Music issues from idle instruments. Glass shatters in expectation of a heavy rock. The hum of a million wings precedes the flap. There is nothing unusual. Cause & effect are on separate vacations. A new day has begun insisting on its own terms, its own reality.

...& he wondered how much force would be required. Whether the old lady was heavier or lighter than she appeared. Whether she would root herself balanced to the top step or raise one foot & already be leaning. Whether she'd be agile enough to spin & clutch his hand or merely stretch her body out toward the impending floor.

These questions & others tapped his brain as he hid behind the wall, like: how would it feel to watch her fall & what would be the sensation of falling? Yes, his view & hers. To push & to feel the push. To watch her body tumble, & to tumble. To witness death, & to die.

It was almost enough to perform the deed in his mind. It was almost too beautiful an idea to spoil by trusting it to physical objects, actual movements. How can the two states even be compared: the real & the imagined? He had killed her a thousand times in dreams, in a thousand different ways, without remorse, without guilt. The act could only be disappointing. Yet, she stands at the top of the stairs, on the ledge, almost begging to prove him wrong. She hesitates like a challenge, & a trembling hand reaches slowly out from the darkness. There is a moment's struggle, then it ends.

Charles Baudelaire drowned between the years 1821 & 1867. Edgar Allen Poe drowned between the years 1809 & 1849. Though occupying very separate continents, they shared the same black water. Not the salty-eyed Atlantic which wept at their sinking, but those rivers that flow eternally from the dank sewers of the soul. Poe was more than an exercise in translation for Baudelaire, he was proof positive of a kindred spirit involved with the alchemy of transforming base Nature into sublime Art. Here was agreement that the Age of Reason was a self-destructive delusion; that there are other powerful forces in human beings that can cause us to act; that there are no objective rules deciding absolute Truth or Beauty; that behind every light there lurks one shadow or more. Baudelaire leaned toward the horrific, sexual & satanic as means of transcending ordinary concepts of reality in order to free himself from the chains of dull society & revitalize life & literature. His attempt was not the simple cliché of turning a sow's ear into a silk purse but to present the sow's ear *as it is,* with its own identity & beauty. The world had to be admitted whole, not in selective part. Plato inhabited by the imp of the perverse. Angels wrestling with demons. Visionaries locked in the jaws of lamprey death.

That sad & glorious drowning.

These slaves (as slaves go) are of fine lineage. They are a credit to their class as well as a brilliant reflection of a master's total control & power. There is, in fact, no finer example of servitude in the long history of the world. The evidence is easily observed. Men, women & children work diligently, farming the land to produce the finest grains, fruits & vegetables. Livestock are kept plump & fertile. Eggs are gathered from rows of clucking hens & butter is churned from the thick cream of contented cows. There are no schools, no churches, no forms of entertainment, no artistic pursuits to interfere with the daily chores, leaving ample opportunity for entire families to spend their leisure time repairing the master's roads, public buildings & drainage system.

Wholly apart from their genuine concern & industriousness though, is their total conformance to proper decorum. They are the epitome of servility. They carry themselves in the correct slave manner, walking about neither too quick nor too slow, heads bowed slightly toward the ground, arms & hands hanging limply at the sides; they do no speak unless spoken to (& then, at a moderate level) & are quick to react to any given command whereby they manage to maintain their station, while simultaneously performing the task.

The master has, indeed, trained his people well. They are a sparkling example to others & much is to be learned & gained from their exemplary conduct.

No one is allowed to enter the master's private grounds, so, at the end of each month, the master's fair share of all goods is apportioned by deputies & deposited outside the main wall of the manor. No one complains & no one questions the ninety percent demanded

103

by the master even though the remaining ten percent is insufficient for the district's population which has a mortality rate only slightly lower than its birth rate. Also, no one questions the wall with its shattered bricks & numerous gaps & perforations. No one questions the amount of produce from previous months & previous years piled, rotting & untouched, on top of the masonry rubble. No one questions the rats, the flies & the horrible stench which pervades the heap. No one questions the dilapidated mansion, the empty courtyard, the charred remains of stables or the fact that the master & his entire entourage deserted the area, left the townspeople to fend for themselves, to be tortured & killed by barbarians some three hundred years ago & never returned.

These slaves are a credit to their class as well as a brilliant reflection of a master's control & power. They are a sparkling example to others & much is to be learned & gained from their exemplary conduct.

These slaves are starving & will remain so.

You understand the difference. Profanity used as a thoughtless comment & profanity used to make a point, to emphasize, to shock, to define a particular character, to break social laws, to announce change or even as a rhythmical device or musical beat. Improper use & changing social values can destroy its effectiveness. There's the story of a group of radical artist-types who used to frequent various respectable restaurants or cafés. This way back when. They'd order coffee, sit politely for a few minutes, then one of the group would suddenly rise & shout, "DAMN!" *Damn?* This outburst would cause proper ladies to faint & fall to the floor, gentlemen to be outraged & staff & management to scramble for smelling salts & the police. The group was soon banned from most eating establishments in the city.

If Ezra Pound were to try this stunt today, he would likely be ignored, or if he persisted & became a nuisance, probably some sweet, grey-haired grandmother would tell him to fuck off. Profanity in itself is no guarantee anymore of a knee-jerk reaction. One must manipulate it like any other language. & if one is uncomfortable with profanity but uses it anyway then one's writing is doomed. The words appear half-dressed with qualifiers & apologies when they need to be stark naked, their genitals exposed, perhaps painted red, white & blue. Made worse when the writer comes to read their words aloud & mumbles through the naughty bits, depriving them of any worthwhile cause & effect. The audience merely shares the embarrassment of the writer & misses the point of the text.

There must be a need & a purpose & an attempt to do something new. If one intends to moon the audience,

one had better have a firecracker up the ass 'cause it's been done before, baby, & nobody's buyin'.

Fuck. I hate that word: FUCK. It begins like a deflating beach ball, *fff... etc.*, ends like a collapsed fish bone, *et cetera... ck-ck-ck-ck*, while the middle grunts like a fat sow giving birth to quintuplets, *et cetera...* uh-uh-uh-uh... *et cetera*. Fuck. I hate that word. It doesn't sound like what it means. Fuck. Or maybe it does. Fuck. But it's useful: to surprise-fuck, to embarrass-fuck, to shock-fuck, to impress-upon-fuck, to make-a-point-fuck. That is, for a writer-fuck, it's useful-fuck. So I'm getting-used-to-it-fuck. Saying-it-more-often-fuck. Fuck, fuck. Getting-less-upset-fuck. Learning-to-laugh-at-it-fuck. Fuck, fuck, fuckity-fuck-fuck. Fuckity-fuck-fuck-fuck. That's the ticket-fuck! Fuckity-fuckity-HAHA-fuck. FOO-KITTY, FOO-FOO (I'm cheating-fuck). Fuck, fuck. Fuck, fuck, fuck. Hilarious-fuck. HAHA-fuck. HAHA-fuckity-fuck-fuck. It's just-a-word-fuck. Just a four-letter-word-fuck. Like *word*, like *like*: like/fuck, like/word/fuck, word/like/fuck, fuck/like/word (I think I'm winning-fuck). Sing it out-fuck! Fuck, fuck, fuck, fuck, fuck. Fuck, fuck, fuck, fuck. Like, big-deal-fuck. Like, it's just-a-word-fuck. Like who-cares-fuck. Not me. I don't give a fuck. FUCK can go fuck-up-a-rope or take a flyin'-fuckin'-leap for all I fucking care. Fuck it. I'm fucking

through bein' fucked up by a fucking word. It's fucking over. Fuck is fucked up as far as I'm fucking concerned. It's fucking through fucking me around. It's *FUCK* for fucking-me for now fucking-on fucking-trippingly off the fucking tongue. I've got the final fucking word fucking now & this is fucking it: FUCK! Fuck yourself 'cause you're fucking finished for fuck sake. Fucking right.

Got two poems accepted by a magazine. *Hooray*! Think I'll celebrate; take myself out on the town; maybe catch a flick. If I get to work with a bit of a heavy head tomorrow, no problem—the boss is on holiday.

I refuse to be one of those writers who writes about being a writer unable to write. I've gone through that lie. I was made to believe that it was all right to allow the craft to sail rudderless since there was no possible way of determining a suitable destination. Meanwhile, the contradiction lay in front of me in the forms of books. Whether suitable or not, the books, the stories (as much as they were the voyages), were the destinations. My heroes—Kafka, Cortazar, Miller, all complaining about not being able to write; blaming language for its inability to convey emotions & ideas; falling into silence as a more convincing alternative, then, to arrive at all these books! In denying language & their own abilities to communicate & produce, they accomplish both. Perhaps the work is flawed & incomplete, but if the work fails, it is on a grand scale & the silence speaks well of it. There are no apologies. These writers write about writers unable to write in order to write. They flaunt their character's imperfections in order not to distance the reader, the notion of *artist* still carrying with it those connotations of *god* or *egomaniac* or *alien*.

Having made my peace, I admit to the same or similar problems & goals. The process, the trip, the *getting there* is not half the fun but all of it. Whatever I say is only part of what I want to say & less of what I mean to say. Also more. Jack Spicer wrote, "A really perfect poem has an infinitely small vocabulary." Which makes silence important. The black lines ghosting under inspection. I will be honest: the writer in the story who is unable to write is not me. Still, we dance to the same strange music & there is a Doppler effect which cannot be ignored. From accelerating distance, we wave.

It's time again. Time to relive someone else's past. I smoke... what? Galoises, Gitanes, Marlboro? I drink vodka cold from the fridge & put on some cool jazz. Who am I trying to kid? Whose life is this? I don't smoke. I don't like straight vodka out of the fridge & the jazz is worn & scratchy, almost inaudible. Stranger still, it feels more & more real, as if the artificial was a link between parallel worlds. Another drag, another swig & the burn disappears. Big Maceo croons a number clear from the spinning, black wax, *"Someday baby, I ain't gonna worry my life, anymore..."* Nothing artificial. No links. No parallel worlds. Everything is the one & the one is the other & I am in a groove & the words are practically writing themselves & it doesn't matter whose words or whose images or whose voice I shall be compared to this time— I am myself writing through the ether.

We are all grave robbers. We are all Shakespeare. Sing it Maceo, *"Now I'm in prison but I've almost did my time. Now I'm in prison but I've almost did my time. They give me six months but I had to work out nine."*

It's not something I particularly *want* to do. In fact, most times I'd prefer not to, but... let's face it: everyone has quirks, everyone has their own *thing* that they do that's best left unexplained. I mean, some people see a coin, they gotta flip it. It is not a casual act. It is born of necessity. As for me, I climb things: curbs, chairs, boxes, trees, books, stairs, tables, counters, desks, cars, garbage cans, fire hydrants, mailboxes, toilets...well, you get the idea, I climb everything. If it's above ground level, from a candy wrapper to a snow-covered peak, I climb it. & it simply isn't a matter of wanting to go over something, or around something, or to get at something, I go out of my way to get on top of a thing & look down. Why? There is absolutely no logical reason that I can see to account for my behaviour. I mean, sometimes I get carried away & climb something that's really tall & consequently, really dangerous. Believe me, it's no big thrill finding yourself swaying in the breeze, frantically clutching the polished top of a fifty foot flag pole (especially if it happens to be attached to a twenty storey building). The fact is, I'm scared shitless. Climbing down a thing is not my forté. I can't even use that fine old saw, *I climb a thing because it's there*. There's more to it than that. Even superficially there's more to it in that, not only is it *there*, but I'm *here*. Why should some inanimate son-of-a-bitch chair have something over me? What gives it the right to dominate that particular position instead of me? After all, I am a sentient being with language & a mind (maybe even a soul). So I bloody well make up my mind to climb the thing & look down on it. But that's not it either. The answer I mean. I could as easily look down on it from some other position (a sink or a windowsill,

say). No. There's something about climbing that particular chair, sitting in that particular position which disappears once it has been climbed. Like our coin-flipping friend. He finds it, he flips it, & for a single sparkling moment, it rises & spins like some wild exhibition ride; twisting, arcing, reflecting the light—it magically defies gravity & exists as some new thing, something other-than-itself. When it lands back in his palm, the ride is over, the magic disappears & the coin is thrust roughly into the darkest region of his pocket, there until it drills a hole & escapes down his pant leg for all he cares. THAT COIN HAS BEEN FLIPPED!

Well, it's the same thing with me. That chair has got to be climbed, damn it, & no one/nothing is going to stop me. I march to the chair, step up, balance on the arms, waver, extend my body upright, survey the entire area from my newly acquired position & look down. *God is in heaven & all's well with the world!* I smile. I breathe. "Fuck you chair," I say.

Then the ride abruptly ends & I am trapped high in the middle of a room supported on the frail arms of a rickety old chair. Paralyzed with fear, embarrassed, I picture myself splattered like an overripe watermelon against the hard ceramic floor & wonder what the hell I'm doing here?

It is her & me now. Me & her. Me, her, him & a little one. Goddamn. Goddamn & pain. The phone rings,
we dangle each to an end & emote into the lopped tentacle of an octopus. Rrrrrring! Rrrrrrrriiinng! I place the
cold thing to my ear: love you, love you, beautiful, want,
need, trembling, tell me, wet pants, make it hard, the only
one, tell me, tell me... words pouring into the suction cup
of the dead tentacle imagining warm, soft ear. Lick, kiss.
We crazy goddamn. For sure. Love unreasonable, unfair.
Crazy. Crazy in love. Dangling. We sweat, we tremble.
Urgent. The tiny voice, crying. Goddamn. Goddamn.
Crazy goddamn.

THE TRIED & TRUE WAY TO CREATE A BABY IN THE CANADIAN NOVEL

It happens on the prairies.

The man is married & the woman is a long in the tooth virgin. The man is a well-respected mouse who long ago suffered his fall from grace. He is broken but retains some illusion of grandeur. His metaphor is impotence. The woman is also a well-respected mouse. She has not suffered a fall from grace but her turn is close at hand. She is not broken. Women have an inner strength; they draw from inner resources. These are not explained. They are not required for conception. Her dreams are practical. She wants a career in the city. She wants to be her own person. Instead, she stays around to tend her old, crippling mother. The woman's metaphor is martyrdom.

There is never any elaborate set-up. There is no need. The man & woman are two meteors whose paths are destined to converge. They don't even have to like each other. Mutual respect is enough. Through this, they manage one other thing. He whistles & she is strangely attracted to men who whistle. She has gray eyes & he is as strangely attracted to women with grey eyes. Neither is sure why, but it is convenient. The man wants passion & settles for lust. His own. The woman wants romance & settles for need. Her own.

The event occurs like a badly staged dream. Details can be ignored except to say, she does not orgasm. He struggles & does. When it is over, neither will acknowledge or discuss the act. They talk about the weather. It feels like rain. Novelists are fond of calling this foreshadowing or understatement. This will be the one &

only time the two have intercourse but it will be enough. The fetus will grow like prairie fire. Chemical douches will not kill it. Witches' brew will not kill it. Prayer will not kill it. Odds will not kill it. Where millions of properly prepared conceptions will abort, this child will snub its nose & survive.

The mother will die giving birth, having never seen her child, a girl. The man & his wife will adopt the child & the grandmother (so to speak & still crippling), the grandmother will weep constantly at the sight of the child's grey eyes. The wife will suffer by the intrusion & go mad. The child will whistle in her sleep. The man will drown himself in the river.

Everything is in bud. Funny how a change of weather can make a difference. I hear birds singing outside the window. I put on a sweatshirt & walk out into the morning air. I have a goofy grin on my face. There is a lilt in my step. Yep, the sap is definitely running.

A black bird raises one foot, then dips it casually into the water's edge. The water is still & cold. Bird shivers, but proceeds forward, toward the deep belly of the lake. As it walks, water buries ashen ankles, ascends knees, covers legs & envelopes bird's ebony chest. The mounting pressure resists & slows bird's progress, but on it furrows, parting the surface with methodical thrusts, burrowing deeper & deeper into the reluctant water.

Before it, the water remains cool, pale & impassive. Behind, a black slick foams in the wake of bird, foams & spreads, anointing the surface with a sable dye.

Soon, only the jet-black head & ashen beak remain above water. The inky slick now contaminates every shore &, with the disappearance of bird, the final circle of clear water closes in upon itself, dissolves like chalk against the tide.

Much time passes. Finally, a breath of wind stirs the lake's face, upsetting the stillness, causing waves to pucker & settle like the feathers on a black bird. The whole body quivers, responds to the massaging fingers of wind, rolls & swells, now eager to stretch, eager to explore, clutch & engulf more of the shoreline.

A stokehole moon exceeds the dull horizon, burns upon the restless, surging mass & a vivid orange eye opens in the face of the lake. There is the crack of new bones, the suck of new lungs, as Raven advances, surveying his territory.

Everything goes with the rest. Most won't admit it. You can't separate a chunk & claim it stands on its own, unaffected. You can't expect it to remain absolute. Everything goes with the rest & you can't strip it of all baggage or cleanse it of all impurities. Alice bit into both cookies & the mirror distorted. The index finger is shorter than the middle finger & longer than the pinky, making it both short & long at the same time. Einstein loves his relatives. I say black, you say white. I say in, you say out. I say up, you say down. Alongside each, its opposite. Take a thing, scrub it with steel wool & carbolic, buff it, scent it with lemon & there will still exist that other: blemished, scratched, stinking of tar & collecting fingerprints.

We've gotten it all backwards. The blind man clings to the back of the lame man. There is a sort of comfortable order at work here that neither questions.

"What do you see?" asks the lame man.

"Nothing," says the blind man. "Where are you taking me?"

& so it goes.

I was walking through a park & stumbled onto a base-ball tournament. Teams of women & teams of young girls were playing. I moved from the older to the younger & was amazed at the similarities. I'm not much of a sports spectator anymore but I would have expected greater differences associated with the vast range of age. In bitter fact, the players were strict practitioners of professionalism from their uniforms to their team songs to their desire to win at all costs.

"YOU'VE GOT TO WANT IT TO WIN IT & WE WANT IT MORE!" they shouted in unison. One young girl, the pitcher, actually broke out in tears after an inning that allowed in two runs. The coach was right there with his patented pep talk & the mother of the girl joined the bench to echo the coach. No one mentioned that it was only a game. The stress was on retaliation; on putting the other team down. At the ages of thirteen or fourteen these girls were being prepared for war.

I have seen these people before, these out-of-the-game, out-of-shape coaches & parents who attempt to instill in children what they call a *healthy, competitive team spirit*. These adults were part of my own game-playing youth, but the sports have gotten much larger, more organized & more lethal. With the advent of superstars & super wages, every unfulfilled parent wants to create their own super brat even at the pewee level. Children are being armed with short-term tools to deal with long-term life. They are being cheated of their childhood by being denied the luxury of *fun*. It is sad & also frightening to watch this form of accepted social brainwashing. It is a shame that it emerges part & parcel with the advent of a new concern for health & physical fitness. Clearly, we are

too far in the wrong direction; too caught up in the extreme pressure of *making it*. Being successful to the detriment of others, being trapped in the illusion of *forever young & beautiful* is dangerous & limiting without some form of positive mental & emotional stimulation. Not stimulation that comes from a shot or a pill, but the kind that accompanies broad education, art & love.

It is ironic that some adults earn their living teaching others how to have fun. Why should this needed ability have to be reintroduced (or, more often & more sadly, introduced for the first time) in adulthood?

Picasso said, "I spent all my life learning to paint like a child."

We are all drowning. We do, however, have a choice of water.

The gardens are chock-full of flowers: tulips, daffodils & others that I have no clues as to what their names are. The sun is shining & it's almost warm. People are out walking their dogs, tossing sticks *et cetera*. I look at my watch. Time to meet a few pals for drinks at the pub. I mosey across the grass toward the street.

It happens as easily as this: you walk down the street & into a knife. Someone holds the knife (it doesn't matter who) & you remain standing, posing for a split second, mouth open, tongue frozen, eyes wide as though someone is taking your picture. Maybe you believe you're making the front page or the six o'clock news. You stare at your assailant & your face says something like, "Excuse me, but do I know you?" or "I think you've made a dreadful mistake" or "This can't happen to me; I'm not prepared" or "Not like this, you see. It shouldn't happen like this."

But your voice has been disconnected & the company's gone bankrupt & you realize there's nothing really to say & no one's listening anyways so you simply collapse onto the sidewalk as eloquently as possible under the circumstances, taking your place alongside sacks of potatoes, onions, long-grained rice, rutabaga, candy wrappers, chewing gum, broken glass & torn newspapers. But you do manage to swipe one ripe strawberry on your way down & you bite into it & the taste is warm, sweet & unusually satisfying. Your lips glow a brilliant scarlet, the corners of your mouth dribble red as you turn your head a final time, smile once for the cameras &... "Excellent! Well done! Side view, front view, 8X10 glossy plus convenient wallet size & *that's-a-wrap-put-it-in-a-can-&-we're-outta-here!*"

You've made it.

*You think I have become less of a writer, that I lack my original sensitivity. You make a mistake. If I am less of a writer it is because I have become **more** sensitive. In this way, my time is not my own & I allow others to dictate my life. To be a great writer requires tremendous insensitivity & the courage to act upon it.*

I wrote this a long time ago, & now, I don't quite believe it (but I don't quite disbelieve it either). It's a problem of definition. The old God-trick of being all-just & all-forgiving simultaneously. A writer must be sensitive to the world & others without losing track of the writer. This demands a great deal of selfishness. I admit I have grown selfish. I require solitary confinement, the act of writing being an asocial affair, the words refusing to materialize on paper under their own steam (though I sometimes wish they would), my body craving any activity other than sitting here at my desk, craving any human contact other than my own.

I am being selfish & what a relief to finally admit it! Freud wrote, "If one accepts the punishment for it, one can go on to allow oneself the forbidden thing." I accept! I accept the guilt & the pain & the happy times missed & the befuddlement caused! I accept bag & baggage in order to advance, to create.

I have grown more sensitive. I understand that my actions may appear rude & odd to friends & family so I bargain. I make pacts because I don't want to shut them out of my life. I want them to know that I love & care for them, even when I am under lock & key. I try to package my time to include the most experiences possible—even those riotous X factors. Including spontaneity. I open myself to the world & if a thing needs doing,

120

I do it. I can't do everything. I do what I can. The drowning continues radiant & magical, without wasted energy, without wasted breath.

&

Traffic roars by my window like a cheering crowd. Where are they going? Where have they been? What special rights have they to wake me with their riotous behaviour & feel no shame? I open my window & call to them, "Listen to me! All of you! You have ruined my sleep with your racket & spoiled a perfectly good dream. Now, I demand either an explanation or an apology. I shall either be entertained or soothed to make up my loss."

The din continues with vehicles & people rushing non-stop, ignoring me & my request. "Which is it to be?" The noise increases, if that can be imagined. Pedestrians duck their heads, mumble into their collars & shuffle their leather shoes smack against the concrete, while drivers conceal themselves behind visors, accelerate & squeal out of sight. "Very well. If you refuse to acknowledge me of your own free will, I shall gain your attention by force." I swing wide the window & step back. Immediately, people, animals, cars sweep off the ground & begin spilling into my room. Men & women hover like models in a Magritte painting gone wild. In fact, most are frantic; pulling at faces & hair, waving arms, gyrating, screaming in terror, fearful they will be struck by an oncoming vehicle or flat-

tened against the wall due to the sheer bulk of converging bodies. For myself, I know there is ample room for all of them—more!—& even unveil the closet & pull a few drawers to calm them.

"You see? Plenty of room. Now please, control yourselves!" The room quiets & except for a few muffled sobs I am able to pose my questions uninterrupted. "So tell me, what reason is there for all the clamour & hurry out in the streets?" No one answers. There is a fidgety silence only, as each person examines the face of their neighbour. "You mean to say that not one of you can offer any excuse to account for your rude actions? That you are all operating to no purpose, mindlessly following the clang of any bell, the drift of any breeze? Am I to believe that not one of you has ever taken the time or the interest to step from the crowd & question your position in it?" The crowd fusses & stamps. It ripples like the tense ear of a puppy asked to sit too long.

"I don't believe it. I've been robbed of part of my life by a roving pack of bellowing corpses, a tangled string of tin can wind chimes. Get out! Get out all of you before you transform to ostriches & begin burying your heads in my bedsheets! Out! Out!" I wave my hands, fanning the crowd like smoke, funnelling it through the window & back into the street. As the last of it disappears I slam the window shut & tighten the lock.

Outside, the clatter begins anew. I reach for my pillow, draw it near my ears, but before I can cover them, there is a silence! The kind of silence that occurs at some raging parties when, for no apparent reason, everything stops for a split second: conversations, laughter, music. Or, the kind of silence produced by a group of playing

children who accidentally discover a dead body in the sandbox. It is that kind of silence where one never knows whether to begin again from where one left off or to fly out in some new, uncharted direction. I sit up, freeze straight as a tuning fork—& wait.

It is not imperative to make everyone your friend. Most people bore me & are not worth the time. I speak against the masses without defining them. Why should I? We know who they are & so do they. They are mainly nice, responsible, productive folk, which is reason enough not to trust them. They cope. They persevere. They endure. They are part cockroach, part shark. At some point, one of them blows a few others away & the rest wonder why. They can't understand it. Until they think. Until they begin to list certain behaviours which, while possibly innocent on their own, add up to a character study of Jack the Ripper & everyone goes *tsk-tsk* & agrees that it was bound to happen, they could even see it coming. Meanwhile, they miss the sounds of knives sharpening in their own attics. It is enough to make one leery of their company.

Actually, it is not the out-&-out killers who are the worst. At least they are easy to spot & provide some excitement. It's the leeches that get to me. They have no real life of their own so they try to share in mine. They

want to consume me under the pretence of good intentions. Nothing to be done except burn them off with the lit end of a cigarette. They call me a heartless bastard. A loner. Perhaps. But in the company of people with similar exceptional energy, a transforming magic occurs & I am considered sociable, almost charming.

There are definite pros & cons to having a pub right around the corner. 'Course, at this point, all my examples are both pro & con, like, "Sure, I'm driving officer. I'm much too drunk to walk." Haha. Good thing I played some darts & ate a dirty burger. No point trying to get any work done tonight. Just take a couple of aspirins & crash. Goodnight.

There is a light behind the ribs that moves me. There is nothing spiritual in this. A real fucking light straight & solid as an I-beam. My feet follow in odd directions. When I say I have no past I don't mean it to sound romantic. There is a dirty stack of sticks alongside the metaphor. Within. What I mean is that my recollections are vague & there are few things that ring absolutely clear & true. The rest is a blend of fact & fiction, barely recognizable to anyone else who was also there & *knows*, yet honest enough in the telling if, perhaps, more fantastic. When someone asks me if I want to hear the truth I tell them, "Yes, unless a lie is more interesting." Nostalgia is a highly marketable commodity these days. No need to hard sell. The lineups begin before the tickets go on sale; before the program is announced. The oldies are back performing the same numbers & earning a thousand times more bread than they did twenty, thirty years ago. Meanwhile, there are artists speaking their concerns for the world today in the language of today who are totally ignored. Why this fear? Science tells us that in the beginning (when we are young), our short-term memory is more powerful than our long-term memory. As we grow older, this process reverses so that at age, say seventy, while we have difficulty remembering what we ate for breakfast, we can remember entire dinners from sixty years ago. In fact, we confuse this afternoon's conversation with our daughter with a conversation that occurred ten years ago & she believes that we are no longer quite all there—going out of our head, so to speak. In fact, we are too much *there* & not enough *here*. The problem exactly. I will relive my past (precisely) when it catches up to me.

The story of a body blown to smithereens except for one foot. The foot is in great pain & is unable to move. The rest of the body appears to be functioning smoothly (to the foot) & the foot runs through its repertoire of former parts: arms, legs, head, torso. It is the case of the *phantom limb* taken to the extreme.

The foot is collected & sent to be identified & buried. It *feels* the handling & attempts to cry out for help. It *hears* nothing. The various hands touching the foot stimulate different memories depending on the gentleness or roughness of the touch. These memories fight or interfere with the foot's desire to communicate. When the foot is placed in the coffin & buried, there is only the numb stimulation of velvet against its flesh. It gives up trying to reach anyone. The foot replays its stored film of memories until the light of each cell dims & blinks out. A kind of living.

Her warning was clear, "His foot hangs, exposed, like peeled sausage above the bed."

How do I enter his room? Like a doctor perhaps, stiffly, professionally. Brush past with an appearance of objective curiosity; grunt, survey, grunt again. Or should I laugh & make a joke? Act as though nothing has happened? No. Impossible. Something has happened. Something has happened &, nearing the door, I'm still

weighing possible alternatives, still rehearsing possible reactions.

The description has been incredibly correct. The foot is hanging. Metal pins, one through the knee & one through the foot, providing support to what resembles a skinned carcass in a butcher's shop window. There is a porcelain glaze as blood & fluids coat the foot. This glaze seeps down to the heel, accumulates & spills over into a metal pan below.

I can't turn away. A sight which, a few minutes ago, I thought would sadden or sicken me, now fascinates me. Circling the bed, my eyes trace the outline of the foot, note the exposed veins & flesh, the weave & roll of muscle, the abrupt coarseness where chunks were ripped away. Toes stand rigid as stones: one, two, three, four— the small toe has been surgically removed, leaving a clean round hole, like a light socket with the bulb unscrewed. Moving closer, my eye studies the hole, parades around the rim, peeks down inside, searches for a hint of blue electric, a pulsating blue power escaping from the open circuit. I want to watch it dance across the bone. I want to touch it with my finger, force my tongue past the blood, crawl deep inside the joint & rock, rock—be lulled to sleep by a sonorous blue hum; charged, electric alive.

It is monstrous to reduce a man in this way. Pare him down. Reduce him toe by toe, then a foot, a leg. Dreams are a dime a dozen & can be bought, sold or traded at any corner store. Gods are interchangeable; one set of beliefs can be as good as the next & a new lover easily replaces an old lover. But what metal hook swaps places with the tender hand? What glass bauble repairs the vision of vitreous humour?

Rimbaud threw away one crutch only to lean on death. Where he died no one knew him (poor bugger), except as a slave trader & gun runner. No one knew the Rimbaud who poemed with his pisser until they lopped it off & he exchanged vocation over vision & blackflies over barflies.

"Never let them cut a part of you off. Let them butcher you, cut you open, tear you to pieces, but never let them cut a part of you off. If you die, that will be better than living with a part of you gone. Better to spend a year in Hell than let them cut a part of you off."

Rimbaud. Brother. Father.

Big night tonight. I'm working on my lines. I have to say, memorizing lines to a play is probably one of the most boring activities in the world. There's no easy way of going about it. All you can do is carry the script around with you & repeat, repeat, repeat, until it's locked into your brain.

It was an engaging sight—their attack—well choreographed, well regimented, but they lacked discipline, were overly enthusiastic about accomplishing my singular death. I watched with keen interest as they marched toward me four-abreast, their weapons positioned smartly, their uniforms sparkling sharp as a set of well manicured nails; buffed & tapered. No doubt, they were lean, crisp & hungry as wolves in winter. & like a pack of young wolves, the thrill of the hunt boiled their blood; they were restless, itchy; excitement coloured their faces, filled their lungs. The front four grinned, hooted, howled, growled their position—FRONT!

They were not alone in their craving though, & the pain of being not-front, not first-to-kill, burned the length of the company like battery acid sucked through an intestine; raged away at the feet of the troops, caused them to increase their pace & focus their attention rigidly on me, ignoring the marching directly ahead of them. They were suddenly quick on the heels of each other, threatening instant collapse, yet maintaining a certain sense of order. The front four fell first & were replaced by a second group which also fell. This group was replaced by a third front four which fell, which was replaced by a fourth front four which fell, which was replaced... *et cetera.* All fell like reverse dominoes, pitching forward then trampled under, slaughtered by the blind boots of their comrades. When the final four achieved the front, they argued over me like a wishbone, pushing & shoving. They raised their weapons & fought amongst themselves, no-holds-barred, one man falling to bullets, two falling to swords. The fourth approached his prize bare-handed, his rifle empty, his sword broken, his

body wounded; tired, trembling.

It was all I could do to keep from laughing as this pathetic final killer hotly sank his teeth into my neck & rapidly drowned in the swift gurgle of my blood.

...& the father drags a boy in one hand & death in the other & the boy is afraid & doesn't know why & the father is afraid & doesn't admit why & the boy grows to hate his father & the father cries at his own failure to make himself understood & the father dies counting his tears in the mirror & the boy fathers a son & the father drags the son in one hand & death in the other *ad infinitum, ad nauseum...*

This is not my story, but the water is familiar.

One woman said, "I love you, but don't worry. It's not *that* kind of love." She liked to role-play. She liked to be threatened & roughed around. Not hurt, but the threat had to seem real; appear possible. She enjoyed being taken from behind. Then she'd turn on the vicious bitch persona, clawing at me, attacking my cock until I got it up again for her to use. She was exciting & had a gorgeous body: full breasts, tight ass, but her most memorable feature was her vagina. She had very little hair & her genitalia unfolded like a cliché straight out of a cheap porn magazine. *It really does look like a flower*, & I stroked its petals. When my brother was killed, she said, "If you need me, come over. Anytime. I'll do anything you want." I saw her that night. We went at it like deranged grizzlies, tooth & paw. Later, she pulled out the *I Ching* & told me to ask a question & she would reveal the answer. Of course, the answer required some interpretation. I told her I wasn't interested in answers that needed me to interpret them, but I would play the game. I dropped the coins & she recorded. After the proper number of throws & some calculations, she said, "There is a movement from a lower plane to a higher plain. Fire. That's a good sign. What was your question?" "I asked if my brother was happy." She was disappointed. She thought the question would have to do with us; our relationship. When we met the next day she said, "You almost broke my jaw last night." We laughed.

When it ended, she wanted to return my book of poems. I said, "I thought you liked it?" She said, "I lied. I never liked it. I never even understood it."

It was *that* kind of love.

One woman approached me at a party & said, you're so-&-so aren't you? & I said, yes I am & she said, we sort of met at an earlier party, did I remember? & I said, vaguely & she said, she wasn't in a very good mood that particular time & was sorry we hadn't been properly introduced because she had heard some interesting things about me & she couldn't talk much now because she was with someone & so she left & she was tall & slim with tons of red hair & a blue dress & over the evening our eyes would meet across the room & she'd smile & I'd smile & at one point she went upstairs so I followed her & waited outside the bathroom door leaning against the door frame & when she opened the door I figured what the hell? I'm a bit drunk & it's all seeming very roman-tic & what's she going to do slap me, scream rape? Besides that energy is at work & it doesn't normally fail me so I leaned in & kissed her & she kissed me back so that was OK & we continued that way for a time getting our tongues & bodies into it until we stopped for air & looked at each other thinking what clever naughty things we are & when the silence became too great we grinned goofily & I said, so what do we do now? & we both laughed & she said, I'm still with someone & I said, I know but you'd rather be with me which was a pretty bravado & romantic thing to say & I repeated it in my head a number of times to get the full effect & I'm sure she did too 'cause it wasn't something someone said all the time, at least, I don't think so. Maybe she heard it all the time but probably not judging from her reaction so we kissed again & she gave me her phone number & said, call me, which led from one disaster to another 'cause we couldn't get it together & instead had weird

conversations on the phone about broccoli & it turned out that all the interesting things she'd heard about me were bad & some were true & some were false & she was curious & figured I was really too nice to be as bad as she had heard & I said, gee thanks & there was more talk of broccoli & we finally would get it together though much later & over very different circumstances & even became friends but that night of the party I ended the night sleeping on the floor alone & later I was able to finish a poem I was working on because of (thank you) her & the magic.

One woman was part of a witches' coven. The white witch kind. They sang & danced, performed rituals & celebrated the changing seasons. It was a joyful communication between their female spirits & the Earth Mother; very natural, very uplifting, very integrating. She made things out of feathers, twigs, stones & shells. Lovely things. She fashioned character masks in order to live out her angels & her devils. She strove to build her strong, inner self which she might be able to depend on & which would guide her through every adversity. She could never quite manage it though. She could never shake loose that little girl who reaches for a second set of arms when her own are not enough to comfort her. She would sometimes phone me when the moon was full or

when the child was hungry or lonely.

"I'm having my period." she said once. "Does that bother you?" she asked.

"Why? Do you grow long hair & fangs?"

I made her laugh, &, maybe that, more than anything, was what she needed, & why she called.

One woman complained that I didn't know how to treat a virgin. She said I lacked concern. She was right. I said one seldom gets the opportunity to practice. When it was over I mentioned something idiotic about the weather. She remained immobile, impassive, staring at the ceiling. I was desperate. My mind was a zero. I stammered on with the worst & oldest chestnut in the book, "It's not very good the first time." I meant, of course, for the woman, me suddenly remembering that joke: what one guy said to the other guy, *The worst I ever had was GREAT! HaHa.*

Her lips were turning blue. She was the one under water but I was the one who was drowning. "What are you thinking," I asked. She stared at the ceiling. I could see the gears working. She was still alive. Her head snapped to face me. "Well...I've decided I'll try it one more time, & if I still don't like it, I'll stop."

That broke me up, man. That really did. *"I'll try it one more time & if I still don't like it, I'll stop."* That tickled me. It still tickles me.

One woman approached me closing night of a play that I was acting in. We had monkeyed around with the magic-game earlier so we weren't complete strangers. There was a party going on now in the studio. She was already a little high. I grabbed a beer & we started to talk. The guy she was with last time was here again. "He's sweet, but he's young," she said. A second guy joined us & he seemed rather friendly toward her as well. He was one of those square-jawed, thick-haired, good-looking dudes & also an actor. He went to get a beer. I said I could feel daggers from two directions. "Three," she said, & pointed out an older, distinguished looking fellow who was a prof at the university. He came over & asked if we wanted to step out for a toke. She went, I stayed with my beer.

When she returned, I said this was her lucky night. Three men in hot pursuit. I was playing it cool. A little competition is healthy, but... "Only three?" she said. Perfect. Everything was unfolding like a well laid out script. We drank some more beer. I had a friend's car for the weekend so, later, I offered her a ride home. I had a bottle of wine in the trunk & she had some hash in her purse.

Her roommate was awake when we got there & the three of us sat up smoking hash & drinking wine. We discussed dance & theatre & Edgar Allan Poe since she was studying Poe. She decided he wrote a particular poem because he was stoned at the time & she sees the same sorts of things when she's stoned. Black birds & women in flowing gowns & skulls: death images.

Her prof (the guy at the party) wouldn't buy it & neither would I.

Death is a big image for Poe. He likes to sit on the edge & dangle his feet. The symbol for death is often a beautiful woman. Cocteau had the same vision. Mind & body are split. The body says, *go for it, she's a doll.* The mind says, *don't be a fool, she's Death.* Poe saw that the body is easily deceived, the passions a powerful force that had to be kept in check. The mind wasn't strong enough. Poe knew from experience. His own passions drove him. The three of us went to bed, finally. Her, me & Poe. She had one of those futons that doubles as a couch. We pulled it out. She asked me to read her some poems from Poe. I did. She decided she was too tired to make it, so we went to sleep.

I woke up first. There was enough morning light without flipping a switch so I rummaged through her library & grabbed a book by William S. Burroughs. I was reading when she opened her eyes. "Great," she sez. "I wake up with a man beside me & he's reading William S. Burroughs." There was a part about boys being "*smooth & green as lizards on the rocks.*" We had wine & banana muffins in bed & she told me the story of how Burroughs & his wife were stoned outta their minds on drugs & decided to play William Tell with a loaded revolver. It was an old story, but interesting to hear her tell it in her own way.

"Mrs. B puts the apple on her head while Mr. B aims & fires. Goodbye Mrs. B. He hits her square between the eyes. Dead."

We made love, then had a bath in one of those big, old bathtubs with the four clawed feet that you can really get into & enjoy. After, we had another roll in the hay since the first time was pretty drowsy & we were much

improved. She said, "We should go for a walk or get something to eat. A friend is supposed to be coming by with some coke. He wants to get a bit ripped, drive across the border & drink some beer. I don't really want to explain." I wasn't sure if she meant explain to me or to him.

The day was a clear & cool April. We went into a Vietnamese restaurant, pooled our resources, ordered two beers & some food. For some reason, it seemed like Christmas (maybe because of the weather, maybe because of the lights hanging in the booth), so we splurged & ordered two Glayvas for dessert. Then we ordered two more & two more (they were pretty reasonable, price-wise, though not *that* reasonable). This was money that was supposed to carry each of us through the week. There was eight bucks left on the table & I said, you take it. She asked if it was enough for another round, I said yes & so we did.

Our conversation was Poe because I'd read him, Burroughs because I hadn't, a play she was directing, lack of money, lousy jobs, the fact that her roommate thought she would have brought the young guy home (tough luck, young guy), our writing & her idea to open up a crepe house. Why not? People have to eat & she's sick of being a starving artist. Besides, she enjoys cooking for people. The whole gamut & nothing trivial. All very important & straight from the heart. It was a chapter lifted directly from the pages of my favourite novels & I suppose I may be held accountable someday, for having life reflect art, & loving it. There was a sort of dream-like perfection to the affair; very literary & very real.

When we made our goodbyes, there were a few words to do with the motion of the planets & the alignment of

the stars, meaning that we both knew it wouldn't happen again. The words emerged comfortably, not forced or false. It wasn't Bogart & Bergman, but it was memorable just the same.

&

Freud said... There I go again. Quoting. Wouldn't it be nice though, to have read enough, experienced enough & remembered enough to be able to speak in quotes? After all, it's been said before by others & better. It also has the attraction of being linked to a famous name, thus making it seem more relevant, more meaningful, more authoritative. The ears prick. *"FREUD?"* The wheels turn & everyone is instantly on guard.

Years ago I had a friend who used to *talk* in song lyrics. I'd ask, are you busy & he'd sing, "I'm just a lonely boy, lonely & blue, I've got nobody & nothing to do." I'd say, let's go out & he'd sing, "We gotta get outta this place, if it's the last thing we ever do..." It was pretty clever for a kid but it soon drove everyone crazy & you wanted to smack him. Anyway, Freud said that people become artists to gain fame, money & beautiful lovers. Not a very complementary image, especially if it's true. It knocks the stuffing out of Muses, demons, angels & Poe's mad worm. It pricks the ears.

This is nice: a glass of wine in my hand, my famous roast-chicken-dinner-in-a-pot slowly cooking away, girl-friend coming over... Too bad I don't have a balcony. The weather's heating up & it'd be nice to eat outside. Ah yes, the good old days when I could BBQ. Oh well, another time. There's the knock at the door.

It seems to me that we are granted only a few rare moments when we may act, not because we choose to, but because we are compelled to. We must seize on such moments with the fervour of a rabid claw, clutching & tearing regardless of protests; regardless of the caution-ings of our *better natures*. Better to charge full steam ahead & have your nose smacked in the pursuit than to reverse-shift & have your entire machinery overload & grind to a crippling halt. At such moments it is unnec-essary to search out reasons. Reasons are either too numerous, too hidden, too inconsequential, too acciden-tal or else so meaningless that to understand would only trivialize the action.

Case in point: I have been sitting in a bar nursing a single drink for the past two hours & now, suddenly, I find myself fatally attracted to a particular woman, who, until this precise moment, had not interested me in the least. What magic has occurred? A change of light? A change of mood? The tilt of her chin? The curl of her

eyebrow? This last sip of scotch? No matter. I am off the bar stool, bull-to-her-flag, stamping at the table.

"Excuse me...but would it be so awful if I said that you are a most enchanting woman & that I would like to spend the night, or at least a great part of the night, with you?"

"Yes, it would."

"Why?" I ask. The *why* storms from my lips, sweeps across the table like a hurricane upsetting drinks, spilling ashtrays, blowing cigarettes & ashes to the floor. Faces flush, hair tangles, hands flap like the wings of frightened pigeons gripping purses, balancing chairs, clutching the billowing necks & hems of dresses.

"Because, you know. Because & so forth & so on & besides & besides & besides..."

The storm dies as the entire affair loses its spontaneity & flair. I return to my stool & order another scotch. The lights dim, the music slows, the woman abandons her table & approaches me. She is smiling.

"Excuse me...but would it be so awful if I said that you are a most enchanting man & that I would like to spend the night, or at least a great part of the night, with you?"

I stare at her. Who is this woman & what does she want? Who does she think she is to proposition me in a bar simply because I'm sitting alone? She's obviously attracted to me, but I find absolutely nothing that attracts me to her.

"Yes, it would." I notice a pool of smoke swirling in her mouth &, behind the smoke, a flaming ball of light, like a comet, rising up her throat. Her mouth constricts like the iris of a laser, focuses its beam directly into my eyes. I blink as a word forms in the purse of her lips, then...

"Why?" she asks. The *why* explodes in a blaze of flame & light, knocking me backwards, melting the ice in my drink, singeing my face & hands, scorching my flesh.

"Because," I shout. "Because, you know. Because & so on & so forth & besides & besides & besides..."

I carry my journal with me at all times, yet the pages remain unblemished. There is something unnatural to me about its construction—its rectangularity, its uniform parallel lines. Returning home from a restaurant, night-club or bar, my pockets are stuffed with napkins & receipts containing words, phrases, ideas, silly drawings & scribbles in every available space. I put them in a manila folder to ferment & breed.

Deciphering comes later, & the job of cutting & pasting the bits together into some sort of cohesive whole.

To tackle rock, one must become rock. A thought solid enough to sink one's teeth into. That pure petrification. Meanwhile, the rock swims in your blood & you pass each other by in the exchange. No ground is gained.

As much as Sisyphus pushed, the rock drew him.

How did my parents find the time to hide the eggs behind the furniture? It gallops past me. No time for any accomplishments, any folly, any recognition of holidays or occasions, any family.

I remember my father collected empty orange juice containers that were in the shape of oranges. He hung them from every kind of tree because he thought they added some life. He painted the rocks in the rock garden blue, red, white, yellow, pink, green using whatever paint he had, painting whatever colour he felt like so long as it was bright. He liked colour. He cut & painted flamingoes, gnomes, animals from patterns ordered through the newspaper. We had pets he threatened to kill if we didn't look after them properly. Then we couldn't keep him away from them. He built a hotel for the pigeons & a resort for the rabbits. He raised chickens in the suburbs until the neighbours complained of the noise & the bloodshed. "You're not living back on a farm in Saskatchewan anymore," they'd say.

Kids liked him because he built things like stilts &

arrow guns; because he set an area aside in the backyard for Halloween fireworks & Christmas bonfires; because he wasn't afraid to yell at the referees. He acted while others observed. I don't think he ever had a friend. He had pals, but once they fought, that was it—it was all over between them. If a boss criticized him or got on his back, he'd quit. I think my dad began to drown at age forty, when he was repeatedly refused work for being *too old*. He thought he'd always be free, white & twenty-one.

My mother always had a job. She was no less a hell-raiser than my father but she knew you needed money in order to survive. She planted the garden & cleaned the chickens & canned fruits & vegetables. She cooked cabbage rolls & pyrogies & borscht & hamburger & spaghetti & wieners-&-beans & when we'd ask what's for dinner she'd always say, "your favourite" & we'd believe her & she'd make it sound exciting & a treat even if it was potatoes & noodles with sour cream dressed in a strange German title which we were having 'cause it was all we could afford. I never knew we were the poor kids on the block all through my childhood. Other kids were always over for dinner because their mothers didn't have time to cook & they didn't cook this kind of tasty-weird stuff & there was always enough to go around.

On Halloween she helped us make our own costumes from a bin of worn clothes & rags she kept. She saved string, cloth, buttons, shiny paper, coloured cellophane, beads—all sorts of junk. When it rained & we were stuck inside being miserable, she'd dump the stuff on the floor with glue & scissors & we'd make something, anything.

Her favourite colours were sky-blue-pink & shit-

brindle-brown. Her favourite expressions were, "So what do you want me to do about it?" &,"You want to cry? I'll give you something to cry about." Her favourite implement of authority was the wooden spoon & more than one was broken across my backside, for which she'd chide me for breaking her favourite spoon & we'd both laugh. If she thought you were right, she'd support you one-hundred percent. If you were wrong, she'd throw you to the wolves. No mercy. If it seemed dangerous, she'd tell you. If you fell flat on your face, she'd say, "You see? That didn't kill you." Or, "It's only a scratch. You'll live." Then she'd kiss it better or wrap it in a coloured Band Aid.

My mother enters water at the deep end always. She swims only if she fails to walk across the surface.

The word came from above. We were given an assignment in elementary school: "Construct, in miniature, using whatever tools & materials you wish, an EXACT replica of any famous landmark, building, work of Art, *et cetera*, to be completed by the end of the month & then to be put on display for Parent-Teacher Week. The works will be graded & judged on *blah, blah, blah...*"

Our little minds folded at this point. Struck blind by the entire world of *whats* (statues, paintings, temples,

museums, trains, planes...) we were not about to move suddenly & unarmed into the shallow specifics of *hows* (how build, how mark, how judge, how present...) I chose THE EIFFEL TOWER (or it chose me since I could see no apparent reason for choosing one thing over another. The name simply appeared through the haze & I grabbed on as if it were a message from God.) THE EIFFEL TOWER: pins, glue, balsa wood; measurements sixty cubits by two hundred cubits on a scale of... yep, it was all there! I gathered my materials, found a picture in the library & headed home. I would begin immediately.

The day before the project is due, my materials (as well as my good intentions) are still wrapped; the glue unopened, the wood uncut. I give the brown paper bag an accusing look & it crumples guiltily. Outside, storm clouds brew a powerful rain soup. I decide to go for a walk, think over the project, & notice that my presence stirs the clouds into a thick, boiling rage. I race back home, determined to work, only to find that my dad has taken over the construction; has, in fact completed it & is now cleaning up.

"You've put a light at the top of the tower," I said. "I don't remember seeing a light in the picture."

A roll of thunder rattles my teeth.

"There wasn't one. But I know that if I had built the Eiffel Tower for all those tourists, I'd've put on a big beacon like this one." He plugs it in & steps back.

He was like that, my dad, never satisfied with copying a thing EXACTLY, he'd have to give it his own special touch: fixing a beacon on the Eiffel Tower,

straightening the Tower of Pisa, molding arms on the *Venus de Milo*. He'd've put a *real* smile on the *Mona Lisa*, you-bet-your-sweet-ass!

Lightning singes the hair on the back of my neck.

"Now, that's the way I'd've done it," he'd say. "That's the way it should've been done!"

I stare at the beacon. It looks comfortable on the Eiffel Tower. Snug & warm. I glare at it like a heavy rain. The beacon merely spreads its contentment like an umbrella, repelling me, bouncing me across the floor, out the window & deep into the flood.

Rimbaud waits for the school bell then parks himself on a large rock in the centre of the playground. Children pour from the open doors shrieking. A group squats in front of Rimbaud & a young girl weaves among the group collecting quarters in a hat. She passes the hat to Rimbaud, who dumps the silver into his pants pocket.

"All right boys & girls, today's story is HOW I LOST MY LEG. Who can guess?"

"Eaten by a lion!"

"That was last time."

"Attacked by a shark!"

"No, we've done that too."

"Blown off in the war!" "Chopped by a cannibal!" "Trapped under a tree!" "Crushed by a landslide!"

"Vaporised by a Martian!" The answers come whistling.

"No, no, no—you're all wrong! All very good answers, but not today's answer. Today's answer has to do with...SCIENCE & THE DESTRUCTIVE POWERS OF REASON." A chorus of *oooohs* & *aaaahs* treat his ears. "Yes. I was in Ethiopia, as you all know, working as hard as only a reasonable man can, putting in slaves' hours for slaves' pay—& I was the boss. THE BOSS! *Tote that barge, lift that bale!* day & night, night & day & when I was exhausted, I continued nevertheless. Finally, my feeble body issued a warning to my brain: *Slow down, or else! Or else?* answered my brain. *HA! Eat cake you bone-bag!* & I drove myself even harder. & so, it came to pass, my leg fatigued & numbed; the veins swelled like steaming asphalt, roared black as lungs, throbbed like the heart of a seething dinosaur. Oh, I was in pain & still I hobbled through my daily routine shouting, *Tote that varicose, lift that leg!* I watched it hourly purple beneath a medical-white stocking till I collapsed & could reason no more. On a stretcher they bore me through the rough jungle & every step a pounding nightmare. Under the piercing rain I slept wrapped & frozen like a TV dinner. Heavy leather straps bound me to my bed to prevent me from rolling out, either by accident, or through a fit of convulsive agony. When we reached the hospital my leg was a pulsing eggplant & the doctor reasoned, 'Here, here or here?'—the cut! He chose the uppermost (a pound of cure being worth an ounce of prevention), & the knife had a fine meal. I woke to less-than-me & thought the ordeal over. IT HAD JUST BEGUN! Before the last burp an objective eye was sizing up the next course! I fled & took my pain with me. & that's THE STORY OF

HOW I LOST MY LEG. What's the moral? Don't let the reasoning bastards take a piece of you. Let them kill you outright but don't let them whittle you down piece by piece. That's what they tried with me & my leg was only the least part of what I lost to their hacking. Any questions? OK. Now, step up & receive your free gifts from Uncle Rimb." The girl who collects quarters opens a brown paper bag & hands out carved obsidian animals, shell necklaces, exotic feather fans.

"Ohhhh!" "Wow!" "Neat!" "Look at this!" "Look what I got!" "Thanks, uncle Rimb!" "Thanks for the story!" "See ya, uncle Rimb!" "Bye!" "Thanks!" "Goodbye!" "Goodbye!" The voices trail across the lawn & disappear at the sidewalk. The girl folds the bag, places it beside Rimbaud. He holds out a quarter & a small, beaded change purse. She shakes her head, no. They stare at each other; she raises her hand & points a tiny finger at the crutches. Rimbaud smiles, hands them over. She places one under each arm. The rubber tips edge out uselessly from her body. She frowns, scratches at the ground, suddenly giggles, grins, raises the tips & bounds across the grass.

"Look at me, Uncle Rimbaud! Look at me! I'm a bird. I can fly!"

"Yes, you are a bird. A lovely bird!" laughs Rimbaud.

"I'm a bird, a bird!" The girl drops the crutches next to the rock. "I can fly, I can fly! Eeeeeee, Eeeeeee!" she screeches.

Rimbaud hops on one leg, flaps his arms & leans his head back. "Awwwwwrrrk, Awwwwwrrrk!" he squawks.

"We're birds. Eeeeeeeee!"

"We're birds. Awwwwwrrrk!"

"Eeeeeeee, Eeeeeee!" "Awwwwrrrk, Awwrrk!" "We can fly! We can fly! We can fly..." & their voices trail off & disappear high above the trees.

Friends used to read my work in order to see themselves in it. They've stopped. They either missed or didn't appreciate the fact that they were displayed in ragged parts rather than *in toto*. They claimed they'd've gotten better treatment had I been a photographer since then I'd've only cut off their heads or feet.

Everyone wants to be kept intact & as they appear to themselves. No one wants their hands given to one character, their walk to another & their peculiar cough to a third. No one wants to be interpreted or cast under a new light. They don't want to be transformed into literature. They want to be recognized.

Picasso painted a picture of Gertrude Stein who remarked, "It doesn't look like me." Picasso replied, "Don't worry. It will."

The more we are identified as *something* or *some type* by others, the more we assume that identity. The shoe fits even if it doesn't.

What a lunatic gang of ugly stepsisters we are, willing to undergo any humiliation, perform any task, if only to be accepted. No matter that the stuffed newspaper permanently stains our feet or that the toes grow back for more as quick as we chop them. Why suffer for years with our noses in the cinders to earn a proper fit when it's easier to accept what is given? Better to lock the ideal shoe in the coffin of our hearts so we may nurse it in our dreams. Better to put the boots to Cinderella & keep her in her place. After all, there are worse things to be than ugly stepsisters. Much worse. Aren't there?

I slip into my shirt & enter the donut shop. The air conditioning is blasting & I'd prefer they'd simply leave the door open & turn on a fan. It's not even the dog days. I find myself a spot near the window, where I can feel *some* sun at least, & flip the bookmark. I'm reading Kafka's *Diaries*. Not exactly most people's idea of light summer fare, but I happen to find him very funny. I open my notebook.

The newspaper he cradles under his arm is a part of him now, sharing many of his features: yellow with age, thin, dry, mottled, brittle, threadbare. Relics of a different age, their preservation depends one upon the other. They remain constant companions, the paper having been at his side ten, fifteen, twenty years or more. The same paper. As close friends, they know each other's strengths & weaknesses, recognize the straw-like frailty of their bodies. They respect each other & do not call on one another unnecessarily. But, when needed, when repeatedly key-punched by a steeled present that attempts to indelibly stamp & rate an individual as it does a coin, the old man will raise his arm like a tollgate & the paper will bridge the past, unfolding one particular day/month/year's news reflecting on the old man's face, softening it, smoothing it, drawing tears from the parched eyes, smiles from the cheeks & lips; drawing years like used printer's ink from the slack jaw & brow. The two gaze at each other like jubilant mirrors basking in the warmth of their own sun-lit memories.

Rejuvenated, the old man carefully refolds the crackling newsprint, ironing splits, saving tatters, then gently returns the paper between elbow & ribs, presses it close to his body, there until such time as the glow again disappears; until his face again drags, tarnishes dull & scarred like an old coin heavy enough to deposit itself deep within his shoulders & raise his toll-arm just one more time. Just one more time.

My grandmother is 97 years old & beyond death. It's given up on her; refuses to take her. She'll go when she's ready. In her own way.

There'll be a long, narrow corridor. She'll be at the far end & will walk toward me. As fast as she approaches, she will grow shorter & shorter. It's a pattern I've been following. Somewhere between me & the horizon she will disappear. Her end will be a trick of perspective. There will be no pain, no fanfare & no mad thrashing.

We were invited to perform Peter Handke's *Self Accusation* at Kent Prison. It's a maximum security institution specializing in murderers, druggies or a combination of the two. It was my first time inside prison walls & I was surprised to see many of these & the barred gates painted bright colours: blue, red, yellow & green. I don't know what the purpose was. Combined with the bareness of the hallways & the fluorescent lights, the total effect seemed ludicrous; a sort of poor-man's surreality.

The cons were dressed in uniform dull green, including caps. As a group, they resembled a failed work project. Putting in time. They smiled & chatted as we walked by, but there was a heaviness in the air that you could feel. Even without the green outfits it was easy to tell who were the residents & who were the visitors.

We were shown the room where we were to perform

as well as a second room where we could warm up. For those who are unaware of the craft of acting, a warm-up involves physical, vocal & mental callisthenics. It can be as interesting as the show to an outside observer. A couple of the inmates joined us in the room & began studying us. That's the word: studying.

We did our best to behave as nonchalant & friendly as possible & said things like, "Hi," & "How's it goin'?" You wanted to believe that there was some sort of security or tacit agreement between sides, since we all knew our place in the system & our reason for being together at this time.

But it doesn't really work that way, as we soon discovered. A bond has to be set up almost immediately & there is no instruction manual handed out at the door. One thing we figured pretty quickly: if we were there to act a play, then we'd better damn well behave like actors.

We chatted with the inmates while continuing our exercises. They asked about the outside world & we asked about the inside. Most of them were aged thirty to thirty-five & had already spent ten or fifteen years in various institutions. One fellow had been hired as a contract killer when he was young & broke. He killed two people & got caught. He was very matter-of-fact about the entire incident & I wondered: he was a killer then, does that make him a killer now? He said he was up for parole soon. We asked if nearby Mountain Prison was the same as Kent & the con said anyone who gets sent here from there gets piped, meaning, the guy doesn't stay in one piece. Mountain is for rapists & child molesters. *Honour among thieves*, I thought.

When it came time to perform, the room was packed.

Anything for diversion, I supposed, but there seemed to be a genuine curiosity & concern for any sort of contact with the outside. On the other hand, there was little consideration given the actors. Maybe they had nothing else to do, but it was clear that this was their time & their space. The fluorescent tubes buzzed. There were no windows, no source of ventilation. The cons talked & smoked. Still, the atmosphere was far from casual. There was an intensity that penetrated the skin. As an outsider you were watched constantly. & this was no idle middle-class phobia. There was a very real threat in such intensity that could be felt. It was something an actor strived for while these men acquired it through osmosis. They may have been unaware of its origin, but they realized its power. If we wanted their attention, we'd have to earn it. The smoke flexed its muscles beneath the light.

The play itself is a monologue for two voices on microphones. There is very little action. We basically used our voices for fifty minutes. Fortunately, the text involves accusing oneself of almost everything imaginable & we figured the cons could relate to the piece on that level. On the other hand it was not your *normal* entertainment. We began. We chanted, sang, mimicked, mumbled & shouted. The conversations in the audience died quickly & we knew we had them. We were on a roll. I had a bit coming up about using & misusing property where I used a voice that was a combination Brando, Stallone & Durante. The cons loved it. They cheered & whistled. It's a reaction you don't normally get from an audience. We went with the energy & (as they say) we knocked 'em dead & they knocked us dead.

We talked afterward & they all wanted to tell us what

they thought the play was about. & they figured it out for the most part & it was heartening to hear. I kept thinking, what are you guys doing in this place? I wanted to open the prison gates & free them; send them back out into the world!

There was a further stage, of course, to the discussion. One con took me aside. He was the entertainment chairman. He said he liked us. He wanted us back. We had to come back. Soon. & since we were now friends, maybe we'd bring some things in with us, you know, or take some things out. Our sound man had earlier been asked if we had any drugs. There was some talk about *kites* & I asked what they were & our sound man said, *messages*. We were on our way to Matsqui Prison & he'd been asked to deliver one.

With our acceptance into the fold, the intensity, the threat suddenly increased. We discovered that most of these guys were constantly wired. The double meaning of the term *con* crystallized. The air was growing heavier. We packed our gear.

Still & through it all, I learned something about performance & acting from these men. More, this was the first time that the safety of the stage, the comfort of the fourth wall, had been completely stripped away. I had appeared naked & vulnerable. It was frightening & thrilling. It was real.

More rejections today. Today, more rejections. Another phrase to strike from my vocabulary, "No one understands." Strike it out because it's true. I grow bored with explanations. If the work speaks, it is some strange language. My brain echoes with it. When I laugh, my mouth fills with mud & ghosts bite my toes. I don't trust myself alone. One head always tells the truth, the other always lies. How is a stranger to know? I remember now, one con asked why we bust our asses acting if it doesn't pay? He said we were crazy. Out there (that is, in the *world*) no one does "nothin' fer nothin'." He said we'd be better off robbing banks. Yeah, we laughed, it's a dirty job but someone's got to do it. He didn't blink, just gave us one of those patented, intense stares & answered, "No fucking way, man. Not me. You guys are fucking crazy."

The bars are cold against my cheek & I wonder when the two of us had exchanged places?

"It's pissing down rain."
"Why do you swear?"
"It bothers you?"
"I just don't see the need."
"Perhaps that's the reason."
"What?"
"I swear because there is no need."
"Bullshit."

I go to see Cocteau's *Orpheus*. The audience is a typical mix, from the ultra-straights to the young new-wavers. I'm always fascinated by an audience; a crowd. I wonder about their individual motives for being at a particular place. I wonder if there is a common bond. Like, why this particular film?

The movie's opening scene is set at *The Poet's Café*. Immediately there is muffled laughter from the crowd. As the movie progresses, we learn that Orpheus is a poet as well as a National Hero. Cocteau has formulated a world where poets have positions of importance, such as diplomats, & are pursued by fans, much like athletes & rock stars. The laughter increases & infiltrates every sector of the audience. They are not laughing with the movie, but at it. It is an uncomfortable laughter & the audience tries to cover it. They succeed partially. Admittedly, there are problems with the subtitles, the translation is poor & the grammar & spelling are faulty. But these are not the reasons for the laughter & I realize that the common bond for this audience is the name *Cocteau*, nothing more. The audience, for the most part, appears to know little or nothing about Cocteau & his work. Perhaps they knew, *foremost literary French figure*, or *homosexual*, or *drug user*, or *shit eater*, but they don't know Cocteau the *poet*, so they are unable to identify & empathize with the character of Orpheus or his situation. The whole premise is too fantastic, too ridiculous, too mad. Poets as recognized citizens? Poetry as a respected & revered occupation? The imagination runs as far as chimeras, unicorns or green-skinned Martians & no further. Even the wet-behind-the-ears-artists & poets from the so-called experimental *Montgomery Café* clique

are in stitches. They malign their own calling; they shit on their own heads.

Why do poets have this romance for failure? How do they expect to make contact with the world when they're busy drowning in their own piss? Cocteau proclaimed above all things, "I AM A POET." He used every means available to him to communicate. He wrote poetry, prose, plays, screenplays; he acted, directed, produced; he painted & sculpted; he travelled; he published philosophical tracts. If he failed any one of these or more, it was in a grand manner & so deserves praise, even if only for the attempt. If he had some success, so much the better. He lived his life unashamedly as a poet & for this deserves respect. Tear him to pieces in the end if you must, but first, entertain his strange music. There are few who ever attempted to squeeze so many notes from such a frail instrument.

I begin to fold the napkin as I rise from my seat.

"What do you think you're doing?"

"Pardon?" I look at the table. The money is there. The wine bottle is empty.

"You paid for the meal, not the napkin."

"I'm sorry. I don't get it." The napkin is halfway to my pocket. I stare at the napkin. I stare at the waitress.

"You're that poet-guy, aren't you?"

"I guess."

"I've read all your stuff. I want that napkin." The napkin is stained with spaghetti sauce. Between the stains are words, scribbles, thoughts. It is your basic couple-of-hours-alone-in-a-restaurant-with-nothing-better-to-do-no-one-to-be-with kind of shit. There is even part of a shopping list.

"Signed?" I ask.

"If you wouldn't mind."

"How could I? A living, breathing fan? While I'm still living & breathing?" I sign the drunken paper & stagger past her tray.

"Good night," she calls.

"Good night. Good night." I fall out into the street; into the crowd. Famous.

As you've probably guessed by now, I have a Woody Allen-ish complex about inanimate objects. It's not exactly a fear (though not exactly *not* a fear, either), more like an extreme distrust. To begin with, I don't believe they are as inanimate as they make themselves out to be, & whether we imbue them with life or they are inhabited by ghosts or they have an actual life apart is inconsequential. They think & they act. They do not intend to kill us (which would be simple), no, they are tricksters who want to annoy & sabotage us enough to

damage ourselves; to go mad but not die.

The notion that we are owned by our possessions & not *vice versa* is no joke. We take care of them. We protect them. We ask friends to watch over them while we're away. We clean & repair them. We dress them up. We even insure them. & what do they do for us in return? They malfunction & break down. They cause us stress & worry. They tie us down. It is not my imagination when I walk into a room & things automatically fall from their shelves. Or that objects cling to me when I approach, then release & drop to the floor. Or that doorways narrow & widen so that I bang or trip myself. Or that glass ornaments shatter before I touch them. You mean to tell me that you've never noticed that the fridge or furnace always kicks in just as you are about to doze off?

What's to be done? I'm tired of being reasonable. They laugh at me behind my back. They laugh at my attempts to rationalize cause & effect. They laugh at my explanations of *natural* causes: drafts, underground tremors, electrical fields, sun spots. I'm tired of that game so I'm playing the other. I attack the bastards! I scream at them. I threaten them. I smack & kick them. They don't care. They enjoy it. So what? I feel better just admitting they exist. Let them laugh. Now I can laugh too! Right along with them. We'll all laugh. No more excuses. No more explanations. Open warfare & laughter. No mercy. No prisoners. Irresponsible perhaps, but free. Totally free & alive!

The camel, as it were, passes through the opening, though it is obvious that the opening can in no way accommodate the camel. The rich man, on the other hand, cannot even force a hand, a finger through the gaping hole.

"How is it that even though I am built to fit this opening & you are not, it is you who is able to enter & exit unhindered?" asks the rich man.

"Oh, it is a simple trick," replies the camel. "I do it to amuse the children, only. My truly great achievement lies in the ability to slip unobstructed through the eye of a needle."

"Indeed!" cries the rich man. "Why, for that trick, I would trade all my wealth & power."

"It's a deal," says the camel, who quickly packs the riches on his hump, leaving the man with just a few rags & a bare, iron needle. The camel steps away as the man makes a number of lacklustre attempts to leap through the needle's tiny eye.

"There's something wrong," shouts the man.

"Of course there is," replies the camel. "In order to perform this feat, one must own nothing at all." So the camel relieves the man of his remaining rags & pins them to a fine, woven tapestry with the needle.

"Now you are set," says the camel. "God be with you!" & with that, he disappears through a crack in the sky.

We sit across from each other—she & I—coldly staring. Two pages in a book we've read & reread. No surprises. If a flower was ever pressed between us, it's long since turned to dust & smudged our features. We sit across from each other—she & I—& hate. Our one passion. Our one excess. Hate. & boy-oh-boy do we. Hate. She raises her tiny fist at me & shakes it. I stick out my tongue— "NYAHH! Hate you, hate you, hate you," she shakes. "Hate you, hate you, hate you, NYAHH!" We don't remember how long. Centuries maybe. Or a day. What's it matter? Who cares? She squints her eyes & bares her teeth, "GRRRRR, hate, hate, hate you!" Long enough for certain. Long enough for sure. Give her the finger. "Take that you, you, you... take that!" She shakes both her boney fists. Long enough for children & children's children. Long enough for that. Her little fists rattle. "Hate you, hate you!" I snap my fingers. "That, for your boney hatred!" She makes a rude sound with her lips like a fart. "Oh yeah?" "Yeah!" "Oh yeah?" "Yeah!" "Oh yeah?" "Yeah!" & so we continue, each one knowing the other's vocabulary, the other's next move. We continue—boy-oh-boy—to hate. Our one passion. Our one excess. Our one bond. Sitting across from each other—she & I—since sometime in the past, to sometime in the future. We will never part. She shakes her lovely, boney fist. I tease her with my tongue, "Hate you, hate you, hate you, hate you, hate to love you, love to hate you..."

We will never part. Never part. Never part.

Laundry day. I'm at the local establishment, getting a kick out of watching folks fill up the machines. It's busy. Full of different people & different languages. I look at the dryers. I notice that next to mine, whole families are tumbling. I see men's briefs, women's bras & panties, kids clothes, baby outfits—even what might be a dog blanket. My dryer seems pretty dull by comparison.

Always travelling from nowhere to nowhere on the back of a grey horse. Shank's mare. The key is never to arrive. Quixote loves his Pancho as I love mine. She cries the heart of it while I fabricate. The same moving madness. What does it matter if a piece of wood discovers it's a violin? A shift in music. A shift in time. The single difference? *Today, coloured strings are provided for the straitjackets.* A line I lifted from a friend. It serves the same function, to restrict, but there is the illusion of freedom; of hope.

It is an easy thing to make a rainbow of prison bars, quite another to hang it among the clouds. The sky hooks prove useless. When a little girl crosses over, it is called Oz. Or Wonderland. Also Hell. I've lost the excuse of youth but not the awe. Shucks, ma'am. It weren't nothin'. Fish in a barrel. A moving target (they say) is hard to hit. Harder. Any animal with half a brain knows this.

&

I love her because she questions me. She refuses to let me simply exist. I must constantly offer myself, my work, up for inspection & thus clarify my position in the human race. Like every Muse, she stands apart from the drowning. Her job is to provide fresh waters, which she does, in abundance. When I surface we assume our human shapes & exchange information. It passes mouth to mouth like wine & we call it love.